Operation Black Lotus: Espionage, Betrayal & Conspiracy

OrangeBooks Publication

1st Floor, Rajhans Arcade, Mall Road, Kohka, Bhilai, Chhattisgarh 490020

Website: **www.orangebooks.in**

First Edition, 2024

ISBN: 978-93-6554-002-4

OPERATION
BLACK LOTUS

ESPIONAGE, BETRAYAL & CONSPIRACY

In the shadows of espionage, trust is
the most dangerous weapon

SREERANJAN MENON T

OrangeBooks Publication

www.orangebooks.in

"In the shadows of espionage,
trust is the most dangerous weapon."

Dedication

To my mother, Ratnakumari Menon, former professor of Sociology: your wisdom, intellect, and unwavering dedication to teaching have been the guiding force in my life. Your constant support, encouragement, and belief in me have profoundly shaped my thoughts and ideas in ways that are immeasurable.

To my father, Kizhakkepat Venugopal Menon, a proud retiree of the Indian Air Force: your life of service to our nation has always inspired me. Your strength, discipline, and unyielding sense of duty have established a strong foundation for my professional journey and my entire life.

To the nameless, faceless intelligence operatives who operate in the shadows: your sacrifices may go unseen, but they are invaluable. You ensure the safety and security of our nation without seeking recognition.

This book honors you, the silent warriors whose secretive work and dedication are essential to shaping the very fabric of our world.

"युद्धस्य कला गुप्तज्ञानं च, राष्ट्रस्य कवचं भवेत्

अदृश्यः यो रक्षति, तस्य शौर्यमेव विजयः"

"The art of war and the craft of secrecy form the shield of the nation.

Unseen is the one who protects, and his courage alone is his victory.

Author's Note

The development of Operation Black Lotus has been fueled by passion, commitment, and thorough research, taking months of diving into the realms of espionage, global diplomacy, and undercover operations.

By evaluating declassified intelligence reports and exploring the nuances of contemporary spy techniques, every aspect of this narrative is constructed on the basis of genuine knowledge.

This work transcends typical fiction; it represents an effort to create a story that is both engaging and rooted in reality. The intelligence realm is multifaceted, constantly evolving, and filled with dangers, and it was this complex, often unseen landscape that I aimed to portray within these pages.

The time spent investigating the tactics and missions of international intelligence agencies, the psychological profiles of former operatives, and the geopolitical strains that influence their decisions were not merely intellectual pursuits; they were vital to fashioning a convincing, immersive setting that reflects the tension and stakes associated with espionage.

From the peaceful streets of Srinagar to the vibrant urban environment of Toronto, from the intricate lanes of Cairo and New Delhi to the tranquil Alps of Switzerland, I deeply explored each locale, ensuring that every detail, tactic, and conflict felt both real and captivating.

Espionage is not simply about thrilling action; it revolves around the fragile equilibrium of trust and betrayal, the ongoing negotiation of right and wrong, and the psychological impact of existing in a world where each action is a calculated gamble.

As I crafted Aarav Menon's story, I made sure that the feelings, choices, and moral challenges he confronts were rooted in this research, capturing the true nature of the shadowy sphere he inhabits.

As you engage with this novel, I hope you will appreciate the results of these months of thorough research, the credible tradecraft, the genuine influence of global politics, and the emotional depth that brings the characters to life. This marks my first foray into fiction, and it has been both a demanding and rewarding experience to shape this story.

I also wish to pay homage to the often-overlooked heroes in the intelligence community, the operatives who, like Aarav Menon, operate in secrecy, frequently without acknowledgment or recompense.

Operation Black Lotus serves as both a homage to their sacrifices and a narrative full of adventure, action, and intrigue.

Thank you for choosing to read this book. I sincerely hope you enjoy this exploration into the realms of espionage, strategy, and the high-stakes choices that influence our world.

Disclaimer

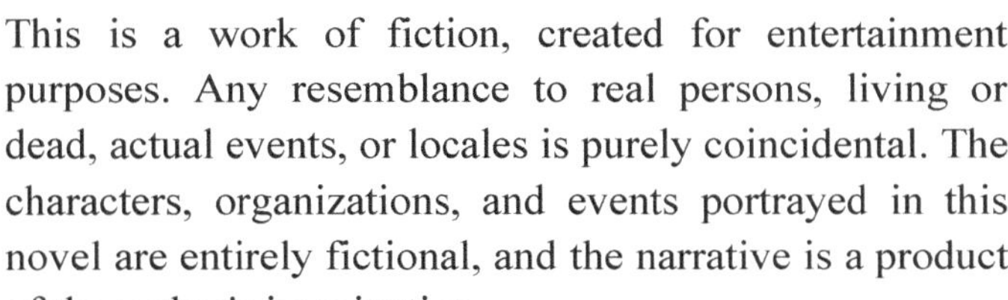

This is a work of fiction, created for entertainment purposes. Any resemblance to real persons, living or dead, actual events, or locales is purely coincidental. The characters, organizations, and events portrayed in this novel are entirely fictional, and the narrative is a product of the author's imagination.

The descriptions of espionage techniques, intelligence operations, and other activities related to covert operations are based on general knowledge of the field and are not meant to represent any specific real-world intelligence agency or mission.

The novel does not claim to portray any classified information or actual events involving any intelligence agencies or their operatives. Readers should note that this work should not be construed as a factual representation of espionage or international diplomacy.

Prologue

Shadows in Srinagar

Srinagar, in the throes of winter, transforms into an ethereal yet forbidding landscape. The city is cocooned under a thick blanket of snow, muting even the faintest sounds of life. The Dal Lake lies frozen, its glassy surface reflecting the faint glow of the overcast sky. Distant, the jagged peaks of the Zabarwan Range stand like silent sentinels, their tops draped in pristine white, disappearing into the heavy mist.

The air is biting, carrying a faint, smoky scent of kahwa tea and burning wood from scattered homes, where hearths work tirelessly against the cold. The streets, once bustling with vendors and tourists, are eerily desolate, lined with the skeletal forms of chinar trees whose bare branches twist upward like pleading hands. The city feels frozen in time, each snow-covered alley and arched pathway cloaked in an uneasy silence, as though the land itself holds its breath.

A frigid expanse of white silence punctuated the occasional hum of distant generators. The pale glow of streetlights struggled against the encroaching darkness; their meager illumination was swallowed by a sky heavy with snow-laden clouds.

Winter's grip held the city in thrall, its streets deserted save for a solitary figure trudging through Hazratbal's labyrinthine alleys. Hazratbal a pious and holy place was witnessing a plot straight from the books of history and espionage.

Hazratbal, perched on the edge of Dal Lake, is a confluence of serenity and suspense. The shrine, revered for housing a relic, stands as an iconic symbol of faith. Its white marble facade glows faintly under the dim light of streetlamps, the dome's silhouette stark against the night sky. The grounds surrounding the mosque are covered in freshly fallen snow, their pristine surface marred only by the faint footprints of a solitary figure seeking refuge.

The labyrinthine alleys leading to the shrine are a maze of narrow pathways flanked by ancient stone walls. These walls, weathered by time and frost, seem to absorb sound, amplifying the oppressive stillness. Overhead, wooden lattice windows from traditional Kashmiri homes peer into the darkened streets like watchful eyes.

The occasional flicker of a kerosene lantern from a nearby shop casts elongated shadows that dance across the snow-covered ground. These shadows appear to move with a life of their own, adding an air of foreboding. Even the winds, sharp and biting, seem to hush their whispers as they pass through Hazratbal, unwilling to disturb the fragile tension that grips the night.

Clad in a tattered shawl, Yasir Idris moved with the air of a hunted man. His breath puffed out in frantic plumes as he pressed forward, clutching a weathered leather briefcase like a lifeline. The corners of the case were worn, its scuffed surface betraying years of use. To the untrained eye, it seemed inconsequential. But the seasoned operatives trailing him knew better. Inside that case lay a trove of intelligence-encrypted files, operational blueprints, and financial ledgers that could cripple Zafar Ali Khan's sprawling terror network. For the man carrying it, the briefcase was both his ticket to freedom and a death warrant.

Yasir paused beneath the faint outline of a crumbling archway, his ears straining against the silence. His eyes, hollow from years of fear and deceit, darted nervously toward every shadow. His paranoia was not misplaced; Sarfaraz Ali, Zafar's ruthless lieutenant highly trained operative of the ISI, is leading his hunters in this quest. A black Scorpio SUV prowled the icy streets, its occupants driven by a singular purpose: retrieval at any cost.

Eight kilometers away, the operations room in Srinagar of India's Research and Analysis Wing (R&AW) hummed with restrained energy. The digital map of Srinagar glowed on the wall, red blips marking areas of interest. Around the conference table sat seasoned analysts and operatives, their faces grim. Secretary, Cabinet Secretariat, Balachandra Iyer, the legendary Chief of R&AW stood at the head, his presence commanding.

"Gentlemen," he began, his voice low but deliberate, "tonight, we have an opportunity to decapitate Zafar Ali Khan's network. Yasir Idris, a key asset, has decided to defect. He's carrying intelligence that could dismantle their financial and logistical operations. But his extraction will not be easy."

The room was silent as Iyer's gaze swept across the faces of his team. "Sarfaraz Ali is personally leading the pursuit. They will not let Yasir escape. If we lose him or the briefcase tonight, we lose a year's worth of work."

Seated in the shadows was Aarav Menon, R&AW's most trusted operative and case officer. His chiseled features betrayed no emotion, but his mind was a whirlwind of calculations and contingencies. Iyer turned to him.

"Menon, this is now your operation.

Codename: Black Lotus.

Your mission is to extract Yasir and secure the briefcase. Neutralize any threats, but under no circumstances can the asset or the intelligence fall into enemy hands. Is that clear?"

"Crystal," Aarav replied, his voice steady.

Beside him, Kiara Mishra, the agency's top analyst and tracker, adjusted her headset. "We've triangulated Yasir's location to the Hazratbal area," she said, her tone clinical. "He's moving toward the mosque. The extraction team is on standby, ETA six minutes. We'll guide you in."

Meanwhile, Yasir's instincts screamed at him to run, but years in the shadows had taught him that haste attracted attention. He moved deliberately, his senses hyper-aware of the hunters closing in. A faint rumble of an engine reached his ears, and his heart raced.

The Scorpio emerged from the gloom, its headlights slicing through the alley's darkness. Yasir ducked into a side street, his boots skidding on the icy surface. Behind him, the SUV screeched to a halt. Three men disembarked; their silhouettes framed by the amber glow of a nearby streetlight. Sarfaraz Ali stepped forward, his imposing figure exuding menace.

"Yasir!" Sarfaraz called, his voice echoing through the deserted street. "We've been through this. Hand over the briefcase, and we'll make it painless. But if you run, you know what happens."

Yasir's grip tightened around his pistol, a Walther PPK he'd procured from a shady arms dealer in Pindi. It felt inadequate in his trembling hands, a false sense of security against the AK-47s slung across Sarfaraz's men.

From his vantage point atop a nearby rooftop, Aarav Menon observed the scene through the scope of his suppressed SIG Sauer SSG 3000 sniper rifle. The crosshairs hovered over Sarfaraz, but Aarav's finger rested lightly on the trigger. He waited, calculating.

"Alpha to Base," Aarav murmured into his throat mic, his breath visible in the icy air. "Target is cornered. Three hostiles, armed. Sarfaraz leading the pack. Request permission to engage."

"Negative, Alpha," came Kiara's voice, calm but firm. "Extraction team is four minutes out. Avoid escalation. Hold position."

Aarav exhaled slowly, his eyes narrowing. "Understood."

Below, Yasir took a shaky step backward, his eyes darting toward the mosque. He could almost hear the muezzin's call to prayer in his mind, a beacon of hope amidst the encroaching dread.

"Last chance, Yasir," Sarfaraz growled, cocking his secondary weapon Glock 17. "Drop the briefcase, or I'll drop you."

Yasir's survival instincts overrode his fear. He raised his Walther and fired. The shot went wide, the bullet ricocheting off a wall. Sarfaraz smirked, his finger tightening on the trigger.

Before he could fire, a single suppressed shot rang out from above. Sarfaraz staggered, clutching his thigh as blood seeped through his trousers. The two men flanking him froze, their eyes darting to the rooftops.

"Sniper!" one of them shouted, raising his AK-47 toward the darkened roof.

Aarav's voice crackled in Yasir's ear. "Move. Now."

Yasir hesitated, but the sight of Sarfaraz's men regrouping spurred him into action. He bolted toward the mosque's entrance, his boots pounding against the icy ground.

Aarav descended from the rooftop with practiced precision, his suppressed Glock 19 drawn. In moments, he was at Yasir's side, scanning the street for threats.

"Yasir Idris, come with me, if you want to live" Aarav said, his voice low but commanding. "I'm your ticket out of here. Keep moving."

Yasir nodded mutely, clutching the briefcase as though his life depended on it because it did.

Inside the mosque, a weathered man with sharp eyes ushered them into a concealed chamber beneath the prayer hall. The room was dimly lit, its walls lined with ancient tapestries that seemed to absorb sound. Aarav wasted no time.

"Briefcase," he demanded, extending his hand.

Yasir hesitated before handing it over, his hands trembling. "It's all there," he whispered. "But they'll kill me. Sarfaraz won't stop."

Aarav's dark eyes met his. "Let me worry about Sarfaraz."

Above, the sound of approaching footsteps echoed. Sarfaraz's men were closing in. Aarav opened the briefcase, his trained eyes scanning its contents: encrypted hard drives, a ledger with coded entries, and a USB stick sealed in a bag and a personal diary.

"Kiara, confirm payload," Aarav said into his mic, holding up the USB.

"Visual confirmed," Kiara replied. "That's the key. The extraction team is two minutes out."

Aarav nodded, snapping the briefcase shut. He handed Yasir a slim Beretta 3032 Tomcat, its compact size perfect for close quarters.

"Know how to use this?" Aarav asked.

Yasir nodded weakly.

"Good. You'll need it."

The footsteps grew louder, punctuated by shouted commands. Aarav positioned himself near the door, his Glock trained on the entrance. His mind calculated angles, distances, and possible outcomes. He had been in worse situations, but none with stakes this high.

"Base, this is Alpha," Aarav said. "Hostiles closing in. Preparing for contact."

"Hold your ground, Alpha," Kiara replied. "Reinforcements inbound."

The first assailant breached the chamber, his AK-47 sweeping the room. Aarav's Glock barked twice, the suppressed shots striking the man's chest. He crumpled to the floor. A second man appeared, only to meet the same fate.

Sarfaraz's voice echoed from above. "You think you can hide, Menon? This ends tonight!"

Aarav smirked, reloading his Glock with a fluid motion. "Not tonight, Sarfaraz."

The extraction team's arrival was heralded by the thunder of rotors. A Bell 407 helicopter hovered above the area, its spotlight slicing through the darkness. Rappelling ropes descended, and armed operatives stormed the area, their movements precise.

Content

Chapter 1

The Black Lotus Awakens 1

Chapter 2

The Mask of Normalcy..10

Chapter 3

The Second Meeting in Vancouver....................................28

Chapter 4

Shadows of Betrayal..37

Chapter 5

Into the Lion's Den 55

Chapter 6

The Double Cross..61

Chapter 7

The Enemy Within 73

Chapter 8

The Storm Breaks 80

Chapter 9

The Web Unraveling..85

Chapter 10

The Heart of Deceit 93

Chapter 11

The Silent War 98

Chapter 12

The Silent Echo 104

Chapter 13

The Mastermind Revealed 110

Chapter 14

The Calm Before the Storm 116

Chapter 15

The Master's Game 121

Chapter 15

Echoes of the Past 126

Chapter 16

The Final Blow 135

Chapter 1

The Black Lotus Awakens

The streets of Srinagar were alive with chaos. Outside the mosque, the frigid air pulsed with gunfire, punctuated by shouted commands and the screech of tires. Aarav Menon crouched low, his pistol steady as he monitored the staircase leading to the chamber. In the dim light, he could see Yasir clutching his chest, his breath shallow and erratic.

"Yasir," Aarav said, his voice calm but insistent. "Stay with me. We're getting out of here."

The defector nodded weakly, his fingers trembling as he wiped the sweat from his brow. Above, the muffled sound of footsteps echoed, closer now.

One minute. In a firefight, one minute felt like an eternity.

Aarav glanced at the briefcase beside him, its battered exterior deceptively mundane. Yet its contents, financial trails, coded instructions, and a diary containing a map of Zafar Ali Khan's sprawling terror network were enough to disrupt the most dangerous plans. If it reached R&AW headquarters intact, it could save countless lives. But the price of intelligence was often steep, and Aarav knew Yasir's survival was the collateral.

The remaining men opened fire, their bullets ricocheting off the marble walls. Aarav returned fire with precision, his training evident in the way he moved, calculated, efficient, and unyielding.

"Down!" Aarav barked, pushing Yasir flat against the cold stone floor.

Above, the heavy thrum of a helicopter filled the air, its rotors slicing through the night. A rope ladder descended just outside the mosque's rear entrance.

Aarav grabbed the briefcase and hauled Yasir to his feet. "Move!" he ordered, his voice cutting through the chaos.

They burst through the rear door as the extraction team provided covering fire. Yasir stumbled but kept pace, his desperation outweighing his fatigue. Aarav pushed him toward the ladder, keeping his weapon trained on the shadows.

Sarfaraz appeared in the doorway, his weapon raised. Aarav fired first, the shot striking Sarfaraz's shoulder and spinning him backward.

"Go!" Aarav shouted, gripping the ladder as the helicopter lifted off.

The ground fell away, the snowy streets of Srinagar receding beneath them. Sarfaraz's enraged shouts faded into the distance, and the city was soon swallowed by darkness.

Hours later, Aarav stood in the operations center of R&AW headquarters in New Delhi, the briefcase resting on the conference table. Around him, the room buzzed with activity as analysts worked to decrypt its contents.

Yasir had been taken to a secure medical facility; his fate uncertain but his defection successful.

Balachandra Iyer entered the room, his sharp gaze locking onto Aarav. "You delivered," he said, his tone devoid of the praise most would expect. "Tell me about Hazratbal."

Aarav recounted the mission with clinical detachment, omitting no detail. Iyer listened in silence, his expression unreadable. When Aarav finished, the room seemed to hold its breath.

"And Sarfaraz?" Iyer asked finally.

"Alive," Aarav replied. "But injured. He won't be a problem yet."

Iyer nodded, his lips pressing into a thin line. "We've decrypted the first layer of the files," he said, gesturing to a screen. "It's worse than we anticipated. Zafar's network isn't limited to South Asia. He's coordinated cells across Europe and North America, with Canada as the hub. If these files are accurate, his operatives are planning something big."

"How big?" Aarav asked.

"Big enough to make 26/11 look like a minor skirmish" Iyer said grimly.

The weight of the words settled over the room like a shroud.

Aarav Menon was born into a family with a deep connection to service and duty. His father, Colonel Krishna Menon, a decorated officer in the Indian Army, instilled in Aarav a sense of discipline and honor from a young age. His mother, Dr. Gowri Menon, a professor of political science, shaped his intellectual curiosity and encouraged a deep understanding of global affairs. Growing up in the shadow of two remarkable individuals, Aarav learned early that the path of duty was not just about sacrifice but also about a deeper understanding of the world's complexities.

Aarav excelled academically, inheriting his mother's analytical mind and his father's tactical thinking. He attended the prestigious Delhi University, where he studied international relations, graduating with top honors. His academic prowess caught the attention of IB, but it was the Research and Analysis Wing (R&AW) that saw potential in his unique combination of strategic insight and intellectual depth. After completing his post-graduate studies, Aarav joined R&AW, quickly rising through the ranks due to his brilliance, quick decision making and remarkable fieldwork.

Despite his success in the covert world of intelligence, his parents, both supportive of his career, had always feared the toll his work would take on him. Aarav, however, kept his personal feelings guarded, rarely allowing his emotions to interfere with his work. But underneath his composed exterior, Aarav often struggled with the cost of his duty. His most personal conflict revolved around his relationship with Aanya Sharma, a fellow professor at the University of Toronto, where Aarav was assigned on a cover mission. Aanya was the one person who saw through Aarav's calm exterior and began to probe into the mysteries of his life, unknowingly threatening the secret he had worked so hard to protect.

The strain between his professional life and personal desires often led Aarav to reflect on his principles. The tension between serving his country and finding a sense of personal happiness was a constant undercurrent in his life. His most challenging moments came when faced with moral dilemmas, moments where his duty as an operative clashed with his own beliefs and relationships. Despite these challenges, Aarav remained steadfast in his mission, understanding that the stakes were higher than personal desires.

In the days that followed, Aarav immersed himself in the intelligence extracted from the briefcase. The fragments painted a chilling picture: encrypted communications between Zafar's network and shadowy figures in Toronto, large financial transfers disguised as charitable donations, and a list of names of possible sleeper agents embedded in Canadian institutions.

One name caught Aarav's attention: Maninder Singh, a prominent businessman in Brampton with alleged ties to Khalistani separatists. His public persona was that of a philanthropist, but the files suggested otherwise. Singh's name appeared repeatedly in connection with arms shipments and recruitment drives.

"Maninder Singh is the lynchpin," Aarav told Iyer during a briefing. "If we take him out, we disrupt their entire North American operation."

Maninder Singh was born in the bustling town of Amritsar, Punjab, during the early 1970s, in a family that balanced business acumen with a deep cultural and political commitment. His father, Mohinder Singh, was a successful textile manufacturer, well-regarded in the community. However, he harbored strong views on the independence of Punjab, which he passed on to his son. Mohinder was an active supporter of the Khalistani movement, often funding local activists and donating to organizations that sought to promote Sikh rights and independence.

From a young age, Maninder was taught the value of self-reliance, both in business and in his political beliefs. His father often took him to the Gurdwara, where they discussed the political struggles of the Sikh people and the historical injustices they had faced. Despite his business success, Mohinder's covert involvement in the separatist cause was a hidden aspect of his life, one that Maninder would only fully grasp as he grew older.

By the time he was in his late teens, Maninder became deeply involved in the Khalistani.

Iyer nodded. "Agreed. But we'll need someone on the ground. Someone who can blend in, establish trust, and gather actionable intelligence."

Aarav knew what was coming before Iyer even said it.

"That someone is you, Menon. Your cover as a professor in Toronto gives you a perfect inroad.

Black Lotus. You leave in 48 hours."

The flight to Toronto was uneventful, but Aarav's mind raced with the details of the mission. He would resume his identity as Dr. Aarav Menon, a visiting Professor at the University of Toronto specializing in international relations. His academic background and measured demeanor had always made him an ideal operative unassuming yet incisive, capable of navigating the murky waters of espionage with finesse.

As the plane descended into Pearson International Airport, Aarav gazed out at the sprawling city below. He thought of the briefcase, of Yasir's sacrifice, of Sarfaraz's snarling face in the shadows of Hazratbal.

This mission wasn't just another operation. It was personal now.

By the time Aarav stepped onto the campus of the University of Toronto, he had shed the skin of the R&AW operative. Here, he was Dr. Menon respected, enigmatic, and thoroughly ordinary.

Colleagues greeted him warmly, students stopped to ask questions about upcoming lectures, and the world seemed blissfully ignorant of the storm brewing just beneath its surface.

But Aarav's sharp black eyes missed nothing. In every interaction, he scanned for irregularities, his mind dissecting every phrase, every gesture.

His double life required perfection, and perfection was a habit he had cultivated to the point of mastery.

Kiara Factor

Kiara Mishra's journey into the world of intelligence was shaped by the harsh realities of her childhood. Raised in the small, politically unstable town of Malda in West Bengal, Kiara grew up amid conflict and uncertainty. Her father, an officer in the Border Security Force (BSF), often worked in high-risk regions along the India-Bangladesh border, while her mother, a teacher, worked tirelessly to provide for their family. Both parents imparted a strong sense of duty, but also a deep understanding of the human cost of conflict. From a young age, Kiara was acutely aware of the fragile line between peace and violence that defined her world.

Tragedy struck when Kiara was just 16 years old. Her father was killed in an ambush while on duty, a loss that sent shockwaves through their family. Kiara, devastated by the death of the man she revered, found herself at a crossroads. The loss hardened her resolve and solidified her decision to pursue a career that would allow her to honor his memory and prevent the kind of violence that had torn her family apart.

Determined to follow in her father's footsteps, Kiara enrolled in the National Defence Academy (NDA), where she excelled in her studies and physical training. However, the grueling environment and the pressures of military life led her to reassess her path. After her graduation, instead of continuing in the army, Kiara chose a different route: she joined the Research and Analysis Wing (R&AW). It was there that Kiara's skills as a tracker, strategist, and combat operative quickly came to the forefront. Her ability to read situations and people, honed through years of observing her father in action, made her an invaluable asset to R&AW.

Despite her success in the intelligence world, Kiara's emotional life remained a challenge. She had grown accustomed to compartmentalizing her emotions, never allowing herself to form deep attachments. The one exception was her bond with Aarav Menon, her partner on the field. Although they had built a professional and efficient relationship, Kiara was acutely aware of the tension between them, a tension that seemed to grow with every mission they completed together. Kiara found herself torn between her loyalty to her team and the growing feelings she had for Aarav, but her sense of duty always came first. She buried her emotions, focusing solely on the task at hand.

Chapter 2

The Mask of Normalcy

Toronto sprawls beneath a cold, overcast sky, its skyline dominated by the CN Tower piercing through the grey mist. The air carries a crisp chill, biting yet invigorating, as pedestrians shuffle through the city streets wrapped in thick coats and scarves. The streets are a mosaic of diversity, reflecting the multicultural pulse of the city. Overlapping sounds of various languages Hindi, Mandarin, Italian, and Farsi create a harmonious cacophony, blending with the distant hum of streetcars on Queen Street.

Toronto was an easy city to blend into, a sprawling metropolis of gleaming skyscrapers and diverse neighborhoods where everyone was a stranger.

Aarav Menon's apartment on Dundas Street reflects the duality of his existence. The building is a modest structure, blending seamlessly with the eclectic mix of shops and residences in the area. From the outside, it appears unremarkable, its brick facade weathered but well-kept, with a small balcony overlooking the street below.

Inside, the apartment is a study in minimalism, yet every detail is carefully curated. A small bookshelf holds academic texts on geopolitics and international relations, interspersed with inconspicuous surveillance equipment. A sleek laptop sits on the desk by the window, facing the street a vantage point for observation disguised as a workspace. The faint scent of freshly brewed coffee lingers in the air, masking the tension that accompanies his covert operations.

The living room's sparse furniture a grey couch, a glass coffee table, and a simple floor lamp suggests the life of an ordinary academic. Yet, tucked away in a concealed drawer beneath the desk are the tools of his trade: encrypted drives, a concealed pistol, and a passport under an alias. The apartment is both a sanctuary and a facade, a space where Aarav balances his roles as a professor and an operative.

Aarav Menon stepped out of his modest apartment on Dundas Street into the cold morning air, his leather satchel slung over one shoulder. To the casual observer, he looked every bit the academic neatly pressed blazer, polished Oxford shoes, and an expression of mild preoccupation.

For Aarav, this facade was second nature. He had lived it for years, slipping seamlessly between the worlds of espionage and academia. Today, he was simply Dr. Aarav Menon, a visiting professor at the University of Toronto, whose passion for geopolitics made him popular among students and colleagues alike.

The University of Toronto stands at the heart of the city, its neo-Gothic buildings exuding a solemn, academic gravitas. Ivy clings stubbornly to the stone walls, even in winter, as if defying the season's grip. The campus is alive with activity despite the weather; students bundled in parkas hurry between lectures, their voices echoing across the open courtyards. The main lecture hall, with its high, arched ceilings and polished wooden benches, feels both grand and intimate a place where ideas come to life against a backdrop of history.

The central quad, a sanctuary of both solitude and synergy, bustled with energy. Students moved with purpose, their boots crunching on scattered leaves in hues of amber and crimson. Some clutched overstuffed backpacks, the weight of textbooks and ambitions pulling at their shoulders, while others balanced precarious towers of binders and notebooks. The rhythm of their footsteps added a percussion to the symphony of academia that unfolded each day. At the edge of the lawn, a group of students huddled together, their animated voices rising above the morning hum.

Laughter erupted intermittently, the universal language of camaraderie cutting through the chilly air. Nearby, the subtle hiss of espresso machines from coffee carts mingled with the scent of cinnamon and cocoa, enticing passersby to pause and refuel. A line of students stretched along the curb, their woolen scarves and beanies adding splashes of color to the otherwise muted landscape. The iconic Hart House clock tower loomed in the background, its chimes marking the passing of each hour with a stately resonance. Beneath its shadow, clusters of students engaged in impromptu debates, their gesturing hands tracing arcs of passion and conviction.

The subjects ranged from philosophy to quantum mechanics, the intellectual pulse of the campus manifesting in every corner.

Further along, the hushed sanctity of Robarts Library exuded an air of quiet determination. Its Brutalist architecture stood in stark contrast to the Gothic Revival styles nearby, a metaphor for the coexistence of tradition and progress. Inside, the soft glow of desk lamps illuminated the faces of diligent students, their eyes glued to laptops and pages of meticulously highlighted notes.

The faint scratch of pen on paper and the occasional rustle of turned pages created a meditative soundscape. Beyond the academic halls, the campus pathways snaked through pockets of natural beauty.

The Philosopher's Walk, a meandering path bordered by bare trees whose skeletal branches reached skyward, offered a momentary escape from the frenetic pace. Here, students strolled in contemplative silence, their thoughts as varied as the fallen leaves scattered at their feet. Near the towering Convocation Hall, a gaggle of first-years gathered for a tour, their voices tinged with excitement and awe. The tour guide gestured animatedly towards the grand dome, recounting tales of the university's storied past and its luminary alumni. The hall itself, with its soaring pillars and intricate detailing, seemed to embody the weight of generations of knowledge. Even the streets surrounding the campus bore the imprint of academia. Bookstores with fogged-up windows displayed volumes of poetry, science, and history, while cafés offered refuge to students engrossed in discussions over steaming cups of chai and lattés.

Street musicians occasionally punctuated the scene with soulful renditions of jazz or folk, their melodies weaving a soundtrack for the ceaseless rhythm of university life. As the sun rose higher, casting golden light over the rooftops, the campus transformed into a vibrant ecosystem of thought and discovery. It was more than a place of learning; it was a crucible where ideas were forged, connections were made, and the future itself seemed to be drafted and revised with every passing moment. The University of Toronto wasn't merely a setting it was a character in the story of all who walked its storied grounds.

Dr. Aarav Menon cut an imposing yet approachable figure as he crossed the bustling University of Toronto quad, his every movement exuding a quiet confidence. His tailored navy blazer hugged his athletic frame, hinting at a disciplined lifestyle that extended beyond academia. The faint glint of his silver wristwatch caught the pale November sunlight as his leather satchel, worn yet polished, swung in a measured rhythm at his side.

There was a stillness to him a poised elegance that drew the eyes of passersby, but it was his piercing gaze that lingered in their minds. His dark eyes, sharp and unyielding, seemed to dissect the world in silence, as though decoding secrets hidden in the chaos of everyday life. To his students and colleagues, Aarav Menon was a prodigy a professor of International Relations whose lectures were revered as masterclasses in intellect and rhetoric. His reputation extended beyond the ivy-clad walls of the university. Think tanks, political circles, and international forums often referenced his incisive essays and groundbreaking theories. But those accolades, like his public persona, were only one layer of the man. Beneath the scholarly charm and razor-sharp analyses lay a life steeped in shadows, a reality he guarded with the meticulous precision of a spy. As he approached the grand lecture hall, the morning bustle began to fade into the background.

The building loomed before him, a monument to learning and inquiry. Its vaulted ceilings and sweeping arches mirrored the ambition of the minds it housed. Aarav pushed open the heavy oak doors, his polished Oxford shoes clicking against the marble floor as he made his way to the podium. The hall itself was a masterpiece of architecture and purpose. A semi-circular amphitheater designed to amplify every word spoken, its walls were adorned with bookshelves that climbed to the ceiling, holding tomes of diplomacy, history, and philosophy. Sunlight streamed through tall, arched windows, casting golden patterns onto the rows of seats where students began to settle in. The hum of chatter filled the space, punctuated by the rustle of notebooks and the faint clatter of keyboards.

Aarav placed his satchel on the mahogany desk and removed a neatly bound set of notes, though he rarely needed them. His lectures were performances as much as they were lessons, weaving narrative and theory into a seamless tapestry that left his students spellbound. He straightened his blazer, his mind slipping into the role of educator a stark contrast to the operative he became beyond the classroom walls. As the final student took their seat, Aarav stepped forward with a commanding presence. The hall fell silent, every eye drawn to the man who had the uncanny ability to make geopolitics feel not only relevant but intensely personal. His voice, deep and resonant, carried effortlessly across the room as he began.

"In international relations, power is rarely overt," he said, each word deliberate, each pause carefully measured. His tone was calm yet laden with an undercurrent of gravity. "It is whispered in clandestine corridors, negotiated in shadowed backchannels of influence. Wars may end with treaties, but they begin long before with alliances, betrayals, and secrets." He paused, letting the weight of his words settle over the room. The students leaned forward, their curiosity piqued, their pens poised to capture every insight. Aarav's ability to draw them into his world was magnetic, his narratives blurring the line between historical events and the stories of people who had lived them.

As he scanned the room, his gaze momentarily locked with a student sitting near the front, a young woman with an inquisitive expression and a notebook brimming with meticulous annotations. He held her gaze for a fraction longer than necessary, a flicker of satisfaction crossing his face before he continued. "The question is can you identify the players before the game begins?" His eyes swept the room, challenging them to think beyond the obvious, to see the invisible threads that tied global events together. Aarav's voice was steady, but his mind, ever the strategist, operated on multiple levels. As he spoke of alliances and betrayals, his own life mirrored the intricate dynamics he described.

The clandestine missions, the dangerous negotiations, the moments when failure was not an option all these experiences infused his lectures with an authenticity his students could sense but never fully grasp.

He began to pace slowly, his hands gesturing with restrained intensity as he wove his lesson into a story. "Consider the Cuban Missile Crisis," he said, his voice rising slightly. "A standoff between two superpowers brought the world to the brink of nuclear war. But the outcome wasn't determined in public speeches or military parades. It was decided in hushed exchanges, in untraceable communications, in the minds of men who understood the stakes better than anyone." The students sat transfixed, their imaginations painting the scenes he described. For them, this was a glimpse into a world they would never inhabit a world of high-stakes decision-making, where the fate of nations rested on whispered conversations and unspoken threats. For Aarav, it was a world he knew intimately.

His life had been shaped by similar moments, where a single misstep could lead to catastrophe. Yet, as he stood before his students, he showed no hint of this internal struggle. His expression was calm, his tone steady, and his demeanor that of a professor deeply passionate about his subject. Occasionally, he allowed himself a brief smile, a flicker of warmth that softened the intensity of his gaze. To his students, it was a gesture of encouragement, a sign that he cared about their understanding. But for Aarav, it was a carefully calibrated tool, a reminder that even in serious discussions, one must not lose their humanity.

As the lecture progressed, he began to draw connections to the present day, framing current events within the same context of alliances, betrayals, and secrets. "The lessons of history are not confined to the past," he said, his voice dropping to a near whisper that made the room lean in. "They are living, breathing entities that shape our world in ways we often fail to see."

His expression turned contemplative, the weight of his double life settling onto his shoulders like an invisible burden. Outside, the world continued to turn, oblivious to the man who balanced on the razor's edge between academia and espionage. For Aarav Menon, the lecture hall was a sanctuary and a stage a place where he could explore the complexities of the world while concealing the complexities of his own life. But even as he walked out into the cold November air, his mind was already shifting gears.

Yet beneath the surface, Aarav's mind churned with the weight of his mission. The Hazratbal mission had left him with fragmented intelligence, but those fragments painted a chilling picture. Zafar Ali Khan's North American network was vast, and its epicenter was right here in Toronto.

Aarav's morning lecture, The Fragility of Sovereignty in a Globalized World, was delivered with his usual eloquence. The packed lecture hall hung on his every word as he wove together historical context, political theory, and current events with the ease of a practiced orator.

"To understand the shifting sands of power," Aarav concluded, his voice measured, "we must remember that the most dangerous enemies are often the ones we never see coming."

Aanya Sharma remained seated; her sharp eyes fixed on Aarav. She was a fellow professor in the department, known for her incisive critiques and a knack for noticing the details others missed.

"That was quite a lecture, Dr. Menon," she said, approaching him, after his lecture.

Aarav smiled faintly, sliding his notes into his satchel. "Geopolitics has a way of captivating the curious mind."

"True," Aanya replied, her tone light but probing. "But sometimes I wonder if you speak from experience rather than just academic observation."

Aarav's hand paused on the buckle of his satchel. He looked up, his expression neutral. "What makes you say that?"

Aanya shrugged, but her gaze didn't waver. "You seem to have a knack for understanding the unpredictable. And you're remarkably well-traveled for someone who spends most of their time in classrooms."

Aarav chuckled, deflecting her observation with practiced ease. "Curiosity and reading go a long way, Professor Sharma. I recommend it."

The faintest smile tugged at Aanya's lips, but Aarav could tell she wasn't convinced.

Later that afternoon,

Aarav made his way to a quiet café near Kensington Market. It was one of his regular meeting spots with Srinivas Rao, his handler and the chief of R&AW's North American operations.

Nestled in the vibrant neighborhood of Kensington Market, the café Aarav frequents is a microcosm of Toronto's eclectic spirit. Its large windows let in the muted light of the overcast day, offering patrons a view of the bustling street outside. The interior is cozy, with exposed brick walls adorned with black-and-white photographs of the city's skyline. A chalkboard menu hangs behind the counter, listing artisanal coffee blends and pastries in elegant handwriting.

The aroma of freshly ground coffee beans permeates the air, mingling with the faint scent of baked goods. The soft murmur of conversations in multiple languages provides a comforting background noise, occasionally punctuated by the hiss of the espresso machine.

Aarav always chooses the corner booth, a spot that offers both privacy and a clear view of the entrance. The seat, worn from years of use, provides a vantage point to observe the ebb and flow of patrons students immersed in their laptops, couples sharing quiet moments, and the occasional outlier who seems just as watchful as he is. The café is a sanctuary for reflection, but for Aarav, it's also a place to quietly gather intelligence, blending seamlessly into the city's rhythm.

Srinivas was already there, seated in a corner booth with a cup of tea. His unassuming demeanor and thinning hair gave him the appearance of a mild-mannered accountant, but Aarav knew better. Srinivas was a veteran of the intelligence world, a man who had survived countless operations through a combination of caution and cunning.

"Anything new?" Aarav asked as he slid into the booth.

Srinivas nodded, sliding a folded newspaper across the table. "Page six," he murmured.

Aarav opened the newspaper to find an innocuous article about a cultural fundraiser in Brampton. Embedded within was a ciphered message, detailing the event's true purpose: a fundraiser for Khalistani sympathizers, hosted by none other than Maninder Singh.

"Singh's hosting a gala next week," Srinivas said. "It's a high-profile event, but the real action will be happening behind the scenes. Arms deals, recruitment plans, financial transfers, you name it."

"And the attendees?" Aarav asked.

Srinivas's expression darkened. "Everyone who matters. Singh's network has deep pockets, and they're pulling in heavy hitters from across the diaspora. If we can infiltrate this, we'll have leverage to dismantle his operation."

Aarav folded the newspaper and slipped it into his satchel. "What's my cover?"

"You're Arjun Nair," Srinivas replied. "A wealthy South Asian entrepreneur looking to support the community. Your invitation will be delivered to your apartment by tomorrow. Just remember, Singh's no fool. He'll test you."

Aarav nodded. "He won't see through me."

Srinivas ' gaze lingered on Aarav for a moment, his expression unreadable. "You've handled worse, I know. But watch your back. Singh's not the only one you need to worry about."

The following week, Aarav arrived at the Brampton fundraiser dressed in a tailored suit, his demeanor confident yet unobtrusive. The venue was an opulent banquet hall, its gilded chandeliers and polished marble floors a stark contrast to the clandestine activities taking place beneath the surface.

The venue in Brampton hosting the cultural fundraiser is an opulent banquet hall, its grand entrance framed by golden archways and elaborate chandeliers. The sprawling parking lot is filled with high-end vehicles, each arrival signaling the presence of Toronto's South Asian elite. Inside, the atmosphere is warm and welcoming, belying the undercurrents of power and secrecy that lurk beneath the surface.

The hall is lavishly decorated in maroon and gold, with ornate silk drapes hanging from the ceiling and floral centerpieces adorning each table. Soft instrumental music tabla and sitar plays in the background, creating an ambiance of cultural pride. The aroma of rich Indian cuisine wafts through the air, a blend of spices that tantalizes the senses.

As guests mingle, their voices form a low hum of conversation, punctuated by bursts of laughter and the clinking of glasses. Aarav navigates the room with ease, his tailored suit blending with the formality of the event. Around him, the walls bear framed portraits of community leaders and philanthropists, reminders of the hall's dual purpose as a space for celebration and subterfuge.

Beyond the polished facade, the fundraiser is a front for darker dealings. Hidden away in a side room, discussions shift from cultural preservation to clandestine arms deals and covert alliances. The opulence of the setting contrasts starkly with the shadowy transactions taking place, a reminder of the dual worlds Aarav inhabits.

As Aarav handed his forged invitation to the doorman, he scanned the room with practiced ease. The crowd was a mix of politicians, businessmen, and activists, all mingling under the guise of promoting Punjabi culture.

Maninder Singh was easy to spot. A portly man with a thick beard and an air of self-importance, he moved through the crowd like a king among courtiers. Aarav waited patiently, observing Singh's interactions and noting his inner circle.

When the moment was right, Aarav approached, a warm smile on his face. "Mr. Singh," he said, extending his hand. "A pleasure to finally meet you. I've heard much about your work in preserving our heritage."

Singh's eyes narrowed briefly, studying Aarav before returning the handshake. "And you are?"

"Arjun Nair," Aarav replied smoothly. "An entrepreneur with a keen interest in cultural initiatives. I've been looking for ways to contribute, and I was told you're the man to talk to."

Singh's skepticism melted under Aarav's charm, and soon they were deep in conversation. Aarav played his part to perfection, balancing flattery with genuine-seeming curiosity.

As the evening progressed, Singh's walls began to lower. He spoke of the challenges facing the community, weaving in veiled references to his more covert activities. Aarav listened carefully; his responses calculated to encourage Singh to reveal more.

Later that night, back at his apartment, Aarav meticulously recorded every detail of his encounter with Singh. The fundraiser had provided valuable insights into the network's operations, but it was only the beginning.

A knock at the door interrupted his thoughts. Aarav opened it to find Aanya standing there, her expression unreadable.

"Aanya," he said, surprised. "What are you doing here?"

"I was in the neighborhood," she replied, stepping inside uninvited. Her eyes scanned the room, lingering on the open notebook on the desk. "You seem busy."

"Just catching up on some notes," Aarav said casually, closing the notebook.

Aanya folded her arms. "You're a hard man to read, Aarav. And lately, I've been wondering if I even know who you are."

"I'm just a professor, Aanya," he said softly. "Nothing more, nothing less."

Aanya's eyes searched his face as if trying to discern the lie. Finally, she nodded, though her expression betrayed lingering doubt.

As she left, Aarav watched her go, a pang of guilt tightening in his chest, his thought was fixated on Zafar Ali Khan. His double life was beginning to crack, and the lines between duty and deception were blurring.

Zafar Ali Khan…

Zafar Ali Khan's story is one of ambition, betrayal, and survival, woven into the political and military upheavals of the Indian subcontinent. Born in the early 1970s to a modest family in the rugged terrain of northern Pakistan, Zafar's early years were marked by conflict. His father, a schoolteacher, was a passionate advocate for Kashmiri independence and a member of a radical political group that sought to disrupt the status quo. From an early age, Zafar was exposed to the harsh realities of insurgency, as his family was often caught in the crossfire between Indian and Pakistani forces, with their home repeatedly targeted by military crackdowns.

At the age of 14, Zafar witnessed his father's brutal assassination by a government-sponsored militia, an event that would shape his worldview and set him on a path toward radicalism. Consumed by grief and rage, Zafar joined a small militant group that had been gaining ground in the region, hoping to exact revenge on those he held responsible. His intelligence and ruthless ambition quickly propelled him through the ranks of the group, earning him the respect of leaders who saw his potential to drive their cause forward.

As he matured, Zafar's vision expanded beyond personal revenge; he saw an opportunity to capitalize on the disarray in the region. His understanding of the political landscape shaped by years of witnessing the instability in Kashmir led him to adopt a more strategic approach. Zafar began working with various international terror networks, including some with strong ties to Pakistan's intelligence agency, the ISI. By his late twenties, he had built a web of connections across the Middle East, Central Asia, and South Asia, trafficking in arms, drugs, and extremist ideologies. His ultimate goal was not just independence for Kashmir, but a broader upheaval of the political order that would allow him to establish a new power base.

In the years that followed, Zafar's network grew exponentially. He became a master of manipulation, using money, fear, and promises of power to recruit militants and corrupt officials. He played both sides of every conflict, aligning himself with various governments and groups when it suited his interests. His reach extended into India, Pakistan, and Afghanistan, as well as into European and North American markets, where he was linked to financing and recruitment for terror activities. Despite his criminal activities, he maintained an impeccable public facade, presenting himself as a philanthropist and a champion of the oppressed in international forums. This dual identity publicly a man of virtue, privately a ruthless power-broker allowed Zafar to operate undetected for years, all while building a global terror network that sought to destabilize entire regions.

The turning point in Zafar's life came when his network's activities began to attract the attention of global intelligence agencies, especially India's Research and Analysis Wing (R&AW). His operations became too large to ignore, and he found himself locked in a high-stakes battle with the very agencies he had once managed to deceive. As his power grew, so did his enemies. Zafar's survival depended on his ability to outwit his adversaries, manipulate allies, and eliminate threats, traits that made him a dangerous and elusive figure in the world of espionage.

The Black Lotus mission was only just beginning, but the stakes were already higher than he had anticipated.

The next show was in Vancouver. Aarav was ready for the showdown.

Chapter 3

The Second Meeting in Vancouver

The city of Vancouver lay beneath a persistent drizzle, its wet streets shimmering under the pale glow of streetlights. The iconic skyline, framed by the snow-capped North Shore Mountains, loomed as a reminder of the city's juxtaposition of natural beauty and urban sprawl. Rain dripped steadily from the edges of awnings, creating shallow puddles that mirrored the silhouettes of towering skyscrapers.

The air was cool and damp, carrying a faint hint of salt from the nearby Pacific Ocean. Streetcars rattled along their tracks, their muted clangs echoing in the mist. Downtown's streets bustled with activity umbrellas bobbed in a sea of pedestrians navigating the city's diverse neighborhoods, from the bustling eateries of Yaletown to the cultural hub of Chinatown. Yet, beneath this veneer of normalcy, the city held an undercurrent of unease, a fitting backdrop for the clandestine dealings Aarav was about to uncover.

The steady drizzle blanketed Vancouver as Aarav Menon stepped off the commuter flight, blending seamlessly with the bustle of the international airport. His dark overcoat shielded him from the chill of the Pacific Northwest evening. Vancouver, with its gleaming skyscrapers framed by snow-draped mountains, appeared tranquil. But for Aarav, this city was anything but serene; it was a strategic battlefield. The enemy's network pulsated through its veins, and tonight, he was set to infiltrate the heart of it.

Maninder Singh's sphere of influence was deeply entrenched here, nurtured by a diaspora of sympathizers and operatives. Singh's fundraiser tonight wasn't just a gathering; it was the nexus of his operations, a cover for darker, clandestine dealings. As Aarav exited the cab outside the mansion where the event was being held, he scanned the area. His eyes lingered on a black Toyota Land Cruiser idling nearby; its tinted windows were too conspicuous for comfort.

"Likely a surveillance team," Aarav murmured under his breath. His voice was picked up by the concealed throat mic he wore, connected to Srinivas, his handler who was in Ottawa.

"Copy that," came Srinivas' response, calm and reassuring. "Keep your wits about you, Black Lotus. This is Singh's backyard. Every move you make is under a microscope."

Located in the upscale Shaughnessy neighborhood, Maninder Singh's mansion exuded wealth and influence. The gated property was bordered by tall, manicured hedges, offering privacy and an air of exclusivity. Beyond the gates, a winding driveway led to the grand entrance, where columns of polished marble supported an expansive balcony overlooking the cityscape.

Inside, the mansion was a showcase of extravagance. The foyer featured a chandelier that seemed to drip with crystals, casting fractured light across the polished granite floor. The walls were adorned with ornate tapestries depicting scenes from Punjabi folklore, while antique wooden furniture bore intricate carvings. The scent of leather and aged wood mingled with faint traces of incense, adding a layer of cultural richness to the space.

The ballroom, the centerpiece of the evening's fundraiser, was a cavernous space with vaulted ceilings and gold-leaf embellishments. Its marble floors reflected the warm glow of the chandeliers, while tables draped in silk held trays of delicate hors d'oeuvres. The chatter of distinguished guests filled the room, their voices blending with the soft strains of classical Indian music performed by a live quartet.

Yet, beyond the surface of refinement, the mansion operated as a hub of covert activity. Hidden passageways led to secure rooms outfitted with state-of-the-art surveillance equipment. Aarav's keen eyes noted these subtle details the extra security cameras, the presence of armed guards stationed discreetly by entrances, and the hushed conversations in corners that hinted at deeper conspiracies.

The mansion loomed ahead, a symbol of affluence and secrecy. The guards at the gate were armed with Heckler & Koch MP5 submachine guns, silent, efficient, and deadly. Aarav adjusted his cufflinks as he handed over a forged invitation to one of them, his body language projecting a confidence that belied the tension coursing through him.

Inside, the scene was lavish but calculated. Chandeliers cast warm light over a crowd of elite business magnates, cultural icons, and politicians. The classical strains of a string quartet provided a deceptive sense of calm, but Aarav knew better. Every smile, every handshake, every toast masked ulterior motives.

He moved through the room, weaving seamlessly into the crowd, his trained eyes cataloging every detail. A flick of his wrist activated the concealed camera embedded in his watch, snapping photos of Singh's inner circle. The images were immediately encrypted and transmitted to a secure server back in India.

At the center of the room stood Maninder Singh, larger than life in both stature and personality. His booming laughter resonated as he entertained a cluster of sycophants. Aarav approached with a blend of humility and poise. The mission briefing had made it clear winning Singh's trust was the priority.

"Arjun Nair," Aarav introduced himself, his voice steady. "We met briefly in Brampton. Your work for the community left an indelible impression."

Singh's sharp eyes scrutinized Aarav before his face broke into a broad smile. "Ah, Mr. Nair! Welcome! I'm glad to see men like you supporting the cause."

Aarav played his part flawlessly. "Community is the bedrock of identity, Mr. Singh. We must protect it at all costs."

Singh's nod was approving but calculated. He gestured for Aarav to join him, and soon Aarav was being introduced to Singh's associates. Each introduction was a puzzle piece: a name, a face, an occupation adding to the larger picture of Singh's network. Aarav's mind worked like a data processor, filing everything for later debriefing.

As the evening progressed, Aarav subtly shifted the conversation to test the waters. He listened as Singh spoke passionately about preserving "cultural dignity" and "fighting oppression." Aarav knew these phrases were coded language, a shield for illegal arms deals and radical propaganda.

"Adapting requires more than just passion," Aarav said during a lull in the conversation. "It requires alliances and resources."

Singh's smile grew sharper. "Ah, Mr. Nair, you understand the game well. But alliances are earned, not handed out."

The words were an invitation, a subtle but clear signal that Singh was willing to test Aarav's mettle. Aarav, ever the consummate operative, responded with a knowing smile.

Later, Singh led Aarav into a private study, closing the door behind them. The room exudes power, its mahogany shelves lined with books, trophies, and photographs of Singh with influential figures. Aarav noted the Glock 19 pistol lying on the desk standard issue for Singh's security.

Singh poured two glasses of whisky and handed one to Aarav. "Tell me, Mr. Nair," Singh began, his tone conspiratorial, "do you consider yourself a man of action or words?"

"Action," Aarav replied without hesitation. "Words only carry weight when backed by deeds."

Singh's laughter was genuine. "Well said! Let me test your resolve."

He slid a folder across the desk. Aarav opened it to find a photograph of a middle-aged man, his face lined with worry. The accompanying dossier identified him as Balwant Singh, a former associate who had allegedly betrayed the movement.

"He's a thorn in our side," Singh said, his voice hardening. "He's been feeding information to our enemies. Take him out, and you'll earn my trust."

Aarav's mind raced, though his face betrayed no emotion. "When and where?"

Singh leaned back, clearly pleased. "He owns a small bookshop in Surrey. Discretion is key."

After leaving Singh's mansion, the streets of Vancouver seemed quieter, cloaked in the stillness of the rain. Dimly lit alleys and narrow roads wound through the city, offering glimpses of neon signs from late-night diners and bars. The scent of wet asphalt mixed with the occasional waft of fresh pastries from nearby bakeries that were just closing.

Aarav moved with calculated precision, the sounds of his footsteps muffled by the rain-soaked pavement. He passed by shadowy figures huddled under awnings, their conversations reduced to murmurs. The rain, constant yet soothing, served as both a cloak and a veil, masking Aarav's movements as he tailed his target.

The contrast between the city's vibrant energy and the subdued tension of Aarav's mission created a surreal dichotomy. Each corner turned, each light flickering overhead, added to the growing sense of anticipation as he navigated through Vancouver's maze-like streets toward the next phase of his operation.

That night, in the sterile confines of his hotel room, Aarav briefed Srinivas on the situation. "He wants me to eliminate a man named Balwant Singh," Aarav said. "The man is likely an innocent scapegoat."

Srinivas' response was immediate. "You can't kill him, Black Lotus. But you also can't afford to refuse."

"I have a plan," Aarav said, his voice firm. "I'll fake it. Singh needs proof, not a body."

The following morning, Aarav drove to Surrey, his Glock 43 pistol holstered under his jacket. The streets were quiet, the shop unassuming. Inside, Balwant Singh was sorting through a stack of books. Aarav approached with measured steps.

"I'm here to help you," Aarav said quietly, keeping his hand away from his weapon.

Balwant's eyes widened in alarm. "Who are you?"

"A friend," Aarav replied. "You're in danger. Singh sent me to kill you."

Balwant paled, but Aarav quickly added, "I'm not going to. But you need to disappear."

Over the next hour, Aarav staged a scene that would satisfy Singh's demand for proof. He knocked over shelves, broke a window, and used a scalpel from his survival kit to make a small cut on Balwant's arm. Blood was smeared across the floor and a scarf, which Aarav photographed before sending Balwant to a safehouse arranged by R&AW.

"Go now," Aarav instructed. "Stay off the radar."

That evening, back in Singh's study, Aarav presented the evidence. Singh examined the photos and the bloodstained scarf with a keen eye. After a long silence, he nodded.

"Well done, Mr. Nair," Singh said. "You've proven yourself."

Aarav inclined his head, masking his relief. As Singh poured another round of whisky, Aarav knew he had passed the first major test. He was now embedded deeper in the web, closer to dismantling it from within.

Back at his hotel, Aarav sat by the window, staring at the city lights. The mission was escalating, and the moral weight of his decisions was becoming harder to ignore. Yet he understood the stakes his actions tonight had brought him one step closer to dismantling Maninder Singh's empire.

The rain continued to fall, masking the silent resolve in Aarav's eyes. The Black Lotus mission was alive and blooming, its petals sharpened to strike.

Chapter 4

Shadows of Betrayal

The early morning air in Vancouver was crisp, carrying with it the faint scent of pine and rain-soaked earth. Aarav Menon leaned against the balcony railing of his hotel suite, his coffee steaming in the cold air. The events of the previous night played over in his mind. Staging Balwant Singh's disappearance had brought him Singh's trust, but the charade was far from over.

The longer he stayed embedded in Maninder Singh's network, the clearer it became that Singh wasn't just a cog in Zafar Ali Khan's machinery, he was the engine of the North American operation. His connections spanned continents, his network of sympathizers well-funded and fiercely loyal.

Aarav's thoughts were interrupted by the buzz of his encrypted phone. The caller ID read Kiara.

"We've got a problem," Kiara said without preamble. Her voice, usually calm and collected, carried an edge of urgency.

"What kind of problem?" Aarav asked, already sensing the answer wouldn't be simple.

"Intercepted chatter from one of our Canadian assets. Singh's lieutenant, Harjeet Kaur, might be onto you.

She's been asking questions about Arjun Nair, digging into your backstory.

Our chickenfeeds are buzzing with activity, they are digging deep, Aarav"

Aarav swore under his breath. Harjeet Kaur was Singh's enforcer, a woman known for her ruthlessness and sharp instincts. If she suspected him, the entire operation was in jeopardy.

"What do we know about her movements?" Aarav asked.

"She's headed to Surrey tonight," Kiara replied. "There's a warehouse there one of Singh's arms depots. Word is she's meeting with an ISI operative to finalize the shipment details. This could be our chance to intercept."

Aarav nodded, already forming a plan. "I'll be there. Get me the layout of the warehouse and the patrol routes."

The industrial district of Surrey, on Vancouver's outskirts, provided the perfect setting for clandestine operations. The warehouse loomed large and foreboding, its corrugated metal walls streaked with rust and rain. A few dim security lights cast faint pools of illumination, creating long shadows that danced across the surrounding gravel lot. The distant hum of a freight train added an ominous rhythm to the scene.

Inside, the warehouse was stark and utilitarian. Rows of steel shelves lined with crates formed narrow aisles, their contents ranging from innocuous supplies to illicit arms shipments. The air was thick with the scent of oil and damp wood, the occasional creak of metal echoing in the otherwise oppressive silence.

Harsh fluorescent lights illuminated a central table where Murshid an ISI operative huddled over blueprints and manifestos. The tension in the room was palpable, broken only by the faint sound of rain tapping against the warehouse roof. Aarav, concealed behind a stack of barrels, observed every detail the way Murshid's fingers drummed on the table, the casual arrogance of Murshid, and the nervous glances exchanged by the guards.

The setting was claustrophobic, the heavy air charged with the threat of violence. Every corner of the warehouse seemed to hold its breath, waiting for the inevitable clash that would shatter the fragile veneer of calm.

The warehouse loomed large in the industrial district of Surrey, its corrugated metal walls stained with rust and grime. The surrounding area was eerily quiet, save for the occasional hum of passing freight trains. Aarav crouched behind a stack of shipping containers, his eyes fixed on the entrance where armed guards were patrolling in pairs.

Aarav adjusted his earpiece and whispered, "Any sign of the shipment?"

"Negative," Kiara replied. "But if they're finalizing the deal, it won't be far."

"Aarav, package inbound". Kiara with an excitement muttered.

Aarav watched as Harjeet stepped out of the car, her posture confident and commanding. She was a tall woman with sharp features and a hawk-like gaze that seemed to miss nothing. Her reputation as Singh's most trusted lieutenant was well-earned, and Aarav knew this confrontation would be anything but straightforward.

Inside the warehouse, Harjeet greeted Murshid the ISI operative, a wiry man with piercing eyes and a perpetual sneer. Aarav slipped through a side entrance, his movements silent as he navigated the maze of crates and machinery. He positioned himself behind a stack of barrels, close enough to hear their conversation.

"The shipment leaves tomorrow," Harjeet said, her voice firm. "Four crates of rifles, two of ammunition. Singh's orders are clear, no mistakes."

Murshid smirked. "Singh's lucky we're even bothering with this. Without Zafar's backing, he's just another loudmouth waving a flag."

Harjeet's expression darkened. "Watch your tone. Singh may answer to Zafar, but here, he's the one calling the shots. And you'd do well to remember that."

The tension in the room was palpable, but Aarav's focus was on the details. The shipment was the key to dismantling Singh's operation. If he could intercept it, it would deal a significant blow to their network and force Singh to act rashly.

Kiara's voice came through his earpiece. "I've got eyes on the shipment. It's being loaded into a truck at the rear entrance."

"Mark the truck," Aarav replied. "We'll track it once it moves. I need to get closer to Harjeet."

Aarav edged closer, his steps deliberate and measured. Harjeet and the ISI operative were reviewing a manifesto, their conversation growing more heated.

"We've already had too many setbacks," Harjeet snapped. "First the warehouse in Brampton, now this. Singh won't tolerate another failure."

Murshid rolled his eyes. "Maybe Singh should stop trusting amateurs. Like this so-called 'Arjun Nair' you've been cozying up to."

Aarav's blood ran cold, though he maintained his composure.

Harjeet's gaze sharpened. "What do you know about Nair?"

"Enough to know he's too clean," the operative replied. "No ties, no past. People like that don't show up out of nowhere. He's a plant for sure, I will wait for cues from Rawalpindi"

Harjeet didn't respond immediately, her expression unreadable. Finally, she said, "Leave Nair to me. If he's a problem, I'll deal with him."

Aarav knew his time was running out. He needed to make his move before Harjeet's suspicions turned into action. As. Murshid turned to leave, Aarav stepped out from the shadows, his pistol raised.

"Hands where I can see them," Aarav said, his voice low and commanding.

Harjeet froze, her eyes narrowing as she assessed the situation. "Mr. Nair," she said, her tone laced with sarcasm. "What a surprise."

"Drop the weapon," Aarav ordered.

Harjeet smirked but complied, placing her pistol on the floor. "You're good," she said. "I'll give you that. But you're in over your head."

"Maybe," Aarav replied, his gaze unwavering. "But you're done."

The next moments were a blur of motion. Murshid lunged for a nearby crate, pulling out a concealed weapon. Aarav fired first, the shot striking the man squarely in the chest. Harjeet dove for her pistol, but Aarav was faster, pinning her to the ground with a well-placed kick.

"Stay down," Aarav warned, pressing his boot against her wrist.

Harjeet glared up at him, her defiance undimmed. "You have no idea what you're up against," she hissed.

"We'll see about that," Aarav replied. He retrieved a pair of zip ties from his jacket and secured her hands.

Kiara's voice crackled in his earpiece. "Truck's marked and on the move. Local law enforcement is en route to secure the warehouse. CSIS will be joining the party soon"

Aarav dragged Harjeet to her feet. "Looks like you'll have some explaining to do," he said.

The industrial warehouse in Surrey reappears, but now it bears the marks of the previous night's confrontation. Bullet holes mar the corrugated metal walls, and shattered glass from high windows litters the concrete floor. The sharp, acrid scent of gunpowder still lingers, mingling with the ever-present smell of oil and dampness.

Outside, the rain creates rivulets that snake through the gravel lot, pooling in the ruts left by vehicles. Stray crows perch on the warehouse roof, their cries echoing eerily in the desolation. Inside, overturned crates and spilled contents reveal the haphazard nature of the retreat. Flashlights from local law enforcement intermittently cut through the darkness as they document the scene, highlighting Aarav's efficiency and Singh's desperation.

By the time the authorities arrived, Aarav was gone, leaving Harjeet and the remnants of the arms depot in their custody.

Back at his hotel, Aarav reflected on the night's events.

The operation had been a success, but the stakes were rising. Harjeet's capture would send shockwaves through Singh's network, but it also meant he would become more cautious and more dangerous.

The next show was in Montreal. Aarav was ready for the showdown.

The Aanya Factor

Aanya Sharma was born to a prestigious family of diplomats. Her father, Ashok Sharma, served as India's ambassador to several nations, and her mother, Sheethal Sharma, was an academic specializing in South Asian politics. Aanya spent her childhood moving between embassies in different countries, attending international schools, and learning the nuances of political discourse from a young age. The constant shifting made her resilient, but it also fostered a deep sense of longing for stability and a home she could call her own.

While Aanya excelled academically, showing a particular aptitude for international relations and conflict resolution, she always felt that her parents' world was far removed from her desires. Her father, a career diplomat, was distant and wrapped up in the world of global politics, while her mother was often preoccupied with her research and lectures. The loneliness Aanya felt in these international cities led her to develop fierce independence.

At the age of 18, Aanya decided to study at the University of Cambridge, where she completed her undergraduate degree in international relations. Her time in Cambridge exposed her to the harsh realities of global politics, particularly the complex dynamics of insurgency, peace negotiations, and the human cost of war. There, Aanya also found her calling: she was not just interested in abstract theory but in the practical implications of diplomacy and conflict resolution. She aimed to bridge the gap between theory and real-world applications.

After Cambridge, Aanya returned to India to pursue her master's degree and eventually became a professor at the University of Toronto, specializing in the geopolitics of South Asia and conflict resolution. It was here that she met Aarav Menon. Despite their initial professional interactions, Aanya found herself drawn to Aarav's enigmatic personality. Over time, she began to notice inconsistencies in his behavior; and something about him seemed... hidden.

She became intrigued by Aarav's ability to compartmentalize his emotions, a skill she struggled with.

As Aarav's secrets begin to unfold, Aanya is torn between the connection she feels toward him and the growing realization that he is not who he seems to be. Her love for him becomes complicated by her deepening suspicion of his true identity. The more she learns about Aarav, the more her own beliefs about loyalty, truth, and justice are tested.

As autumn enveloped Toronto University in a tapestry of gold and crimson, Aarav Menon found himself increasingly drawn to Aanya Sharma, his colleague in the South Asian Studies department. Their paths often crossed in the vibrant corridors of the humanities building, but it was in the faculty lounge, amidst the hum of excited conversations, that the tension began to simmer.

Aarav admired Aanya from a distance, captivated not only by her magnetic presence but also by the way her mind danced through topics like a skilled artist with a brush. He often found excuses to linger after her lectures, soaking in her passion and wit while his colleagues moved on. Each word she spoke seemed to pull him closer; yet, every laugh they shared tightened the invisible rope of apprehension binding him.

One crisp afternoon, while the leaves swirled around outside, Aarav mustered the courage to engage her in a discussion about their shared research interests. The conversation flowed effortlessly, a delightful exchange punctuated by laughter and the energy that surged between them like electricity in the air. As they discovered more similarities in their perspectives on cultural narratives, Aarav felt an awakening of feelings he had long repressed.

Their professional rapport soon blossomed into late-night coffee catch-ups at a quaint café off-campus, where over steaming cups, conversations deepened and the walls of academia began to dissolve. Aanya's laughter became his favorite soundtrack, and Aarav found himself looking forward to those moments when time seemed to suspend itself, leaving just the two of them in their own universe.

Yet, with every shared moment came the gnawing realization that he was treading a fine line. Aanya was every bit the force of nature he admired, but she was also a colleague, and Aarav feared that crossing that boundary could lead to consequences neither of them anticipated. Still, there was a spark igniting between them a chemistry that felt undeniable.

One evening, while they strolled through the university's serene gardens, the setting sun casting a warm glow around them, Aarav finally broke through the invisible barrier. "Aanya," he began, his voice steady but his heart racing, "I know we're colleagues, but I can't ignore the connection we have. I... I want to explore this with you."

Aanya paused, her expression shifting from surprise to contemplation. The moment hung in the air, heavy with unspoken words and possibilities. "I've felt it too, Aarav," she admitted softly, stepping closer. "But I've always been cautious, wanting to protect what we have."

They stood there, the world around them fading to a gentle hum, each heartbeat echoing the weight of their decision. With a shared understanding, all doubts began to dissipate as the reality of their feelings unfurled. They leaned closer, and with a tentative touch, a spark ignited a kiss that melded their worlds of intellect and emotion into a single heartbeat.

In the weeks that followed, Aanya and Aarav navigated their new relationship with the same vibrant passion they brought to their academic pursuits. Their late-night debates transformed into cozy evenings filled with stories of their lives, dreams, and fears, all interwoven with laughter and a hint of mischief.

Together, they blurred the lines between colleagues and lovers, discovering a profound bond that brought out the best in both. They became each other's confidants, challenging and supporting one another in their professional journeys while nurturing a love that thrived amidst the bustling halls of academia.

As the seasons changed outside, their relationship flourished inside, a beautiful storm of intellect and emotion that neither of them could ever have anticipated, yet both cherished deeply. In each other, they found a sanctuary a reminder that sometimes, the most profound connections are born not from ideal circumstances but from the chaos of life itself.

Aarav's life had always been a study in control. His years as an operative for R&AW had trained him to remain calm, calculated, and methodical, whether in the lecture hall or the shadows. But Aanya's presence was like an earthquake, shaking the foundation of his carefully curated facade.

While Aarav's lectures were precise and measured, Aanya's were unrestrained, full of fiery anecdotes and spontaneous digressions that somehow always tied back to her point. Students adored her unpredictability, and her ability to make even the most esoteric topics feel personal and urgent. Aarav couldn't help but admire her, though her unorthodox methods often left him exasperated.

Their professional relationship was a magnet of opposites. In faculty meetings, their debates became the stuff of legend. Aarav's calm, logical arguments clashed with Aanya's impassioned rebuttals, each pushing the other to the limits of their intellectual boundaries. For the rest of the faculty, it was entertainment; for Aarav, it was both invigorating and unsettling.

Aanya wasn't just a rival in the debate she was an enigma he couldn't crack. Her relentless energy, her unfiltered opinions, and her ability to find the cracks in his otherwise impenetrable armor made her different from anyone he had ever encountered. Aarav had built his life around control, but around Aanya, he found himself slipping.

The Force of Perception

Aanya had an uncanny ability to see what others couldn't. Where Aarav's colleagues and students saw a reserved, brilliant professor, she saw something more a shadow in his gaze, an intensity that belied his otherwise composed demeanor.

Her curiosity about him wasn't just professional; it was personal. She thrived on understanding people, peeling back their layers to uncover what lay beneath them. Aarav, with his quiet presence and elusive nature, was a puzzle she couldn't resist. And so, she watched him. She noticed the way his smile didn't always reach his eyes, the fleeting moments when he seemed lost in thought, as if his mind was a million miles away. She caught the slight hesitation in his voice when the topic of security and surveillance came up in discussions, and the way his answers sometimes felt too measured, too perfect.

One evening, after a particularly heated debate on counterterrorism strategies, Aanya decided to push. Aarav had just delivered a clinical explanation of the precision required in eliminating threats, his tone is as calm and detached as ever. But Aanya wasn't satisfied.

"You speak with such precision, Aarav," she said, her tone playful but with an edge of challenge. "But don't you ever wonder about the human cost? The lives, the families? Do you ever feel the weight of it?"

Aarav's response was slower than usual, his composure faltering for a fraction of a second. He met her gaze, and for a moment, his carefully constructed walls seemed to tremble.

"Every choice has a cost," he said, his voice quieter than before. "The question is whether you're willing to pay it."

The room seemed to grow still, the weight of his words hanging in the air. But Aanya wasn't one to let things go so easily. She leaned forward, her fingers grazing the edge of his desk, her eyes searching his face.

"And you, Aarav?" she asked, her voice softer but no less insistent. "Are you willing to pay it?"

For a moment, Aarav didn't respond. The silence stretched between them, thick with unspoken truths. He could feel the danger of the moment how close she was to seeing through him, to unraveling the secrets he had spent years protecting.

"Sometimes, it's not about willingness," he finally said, his voice distant. "It's about necessity."

Aanya tilted her head, her gaze never wavering. She didn't press further, but the understanding in her eyes was unmistakable. Aarav could see it the curiosity, the recognition that there was something he wasn't telling her.

A Catalyst for Change

Aarav knew the risks. Aanya's curiosity, her perceptiveness, was a threat to the carefully constructed life he had built in Toronto. She was too close, asking questions that danced dangerously close to the truth. And yet, he found himself drawn to her despite the danger.

As he walked back to his office that evening, Aarav's thoughts were tangled in the web Aanya had woven around him. She was a force he hadn't anticipated one that threatened to disrupt the delicate balance of his dual life. But for reasons he couldn't fully explain, he couldn't bring himself to stay away.

Aanya Sharma was a spark in the shadows of his life. She could be the light that broke through his darkness or the fire that consumed everything he had built.

And yet, for all the risks, one thing was clear: Aarav wasn't ready to let her go.

Aarav and Aanya - "Unspoken Words"

The first time Aarav Menon met Aanya Sharma, was in a lecture hall at the University of Toronto. He had been invited to speak about geopolitics in South Asia, but it wasn't the content of his lecture that kept Aanya's attention. It was the quiet strength in his demeanor, the way his words held weight without being heavy, and the sharpness in his gaze that seemed to look beyond the surface.

After the lecture, as students gathered around him, Aanya approached, her curiosity piqued. She had heard of Aarav's family background in defense, but it was his calm, composed nature that intrigued her. He was a man who carried the weight of his work, but who wore it with ease. Aanya was no stranger to powerful figures in international politics, but Aarav was different. He didn't wear his authority as a badge; it was simply part of who he was.

Their first conversation was casual, revolving around a question about his perspective on peace-building in conflict zones. Aarav answered with a thoughtful response, and Aanya found herself drawn to him. But as their conversations continued over the months, she began to notice the cracks in his perfect facade. There were moments when his eyes would darken, and she could almost see the burden he carried the unspoken things he kept hidden from everyone around him.

As they began to work together on a research project, Aarav and Aanya spent more time together, discussing everything from academic theories to personal beliefs. Their connection deepened, but Aanya could never shake the feeling that Aarav was holding something back. She became drawn not just to his intellect, but to the mystery that seemed to surround him.

One evening, after a late meeting in his office, Aarav walked Aanya back to her apartment. The cold Toronto night was crisp, and as they walked in silence, Aanya found herself wishing she could break through the wall that Aarav had carefully constructed around himself. Finally, she spoke.

"Aarav, what is it you're not telling me?" Her voice was gentle, but the question was direct.

Aarav paused; his breath visible in the night air. He looked at her for a long moment, his gaze unreadable. Then, with a deep sigh, he spoke.

"Sometimes, the truth is more dangerous than the lie, Aanya." His voice was low, almost weary.

Aanya's heart skipped a beat. She could see the pain in his eyes, and she knew that whatever he was hiding, it was something that had shaped him, something that couldn't be easily shared. She reached out, placing a hand on his arm.

"I don't need you to tell me everything," she said softly. "But I want to be here for you. Whatever it is, we can face it together."

Aarav looked at her, his expression softening. For the briefest moment, Aanya saw a flicker of hope in his eyes, hoping that maybe, just maybe, someone could understand him, despite the darkness he carried.

But just as quickly as it came, the moment was gone. Aarav gently pulled away, a faint smile crossing his lips, though it didn't reach his eyes.

"Thank you, Aanya," he replied. "But some battles are fought alone."

Aanya watched him as he turned and walked away, the distance between them growing with each step. She couldn't help but wonder if their connection, as real as it felt, was doomed from the start. Aarav's walls were too high, and she was unsure if there was a way in.

Over the next few weeks, their relationship grew more complicated. Aarav became distant, retreating into his world of covert operations, while Aanya focused on her work and tried to keep her suspicions in check. Despite the growing emotional distance, Aanya couldn't shake the feeling that there was something she was missing. She found herself caught between two worlds: the one she shared with Aarav, filled with intellectual debates and shared moments of quiet intimacy, and the one she was slowly uncovering.

Chapter 5

Into the Lion's Den

Montreal provides a stark shift from Vancouver's rain-soaked modernity. The city greets Aarav with an icy grip, its cobblestone streets slick with a mix of snow and slush. Gothic-style buildings, with their towering spires and ornate facades, dominate the landscape, exuding a blend of old-world charm and imposing grandeur.

The streets are quieter here, save for the occasional clip-clop of horse-drawn carriages ferrying tourists through the historic districts. Streetlamps, their light diffused by the falling snow, create halos that seem to float in the night air. In the distance, the faint toll of a church bell adds a touch of solemnity to the scene.

The neighborhoods reflect the city's dichotomy. Old Montreal is steeped in history, its stone-paved roads and wrought-iron balconies lending an air of nostalgia. In contrast, the financial district brims with modern glass towers that loom like sentinels over the bustling city below. Aarav seamlessly transitions between these worlds, each step calculated as he moves toward his next objective.

The icy streets of Montreal stretched before Aarav Menon as he exited the train station, his coat pulled tightly around him. The city was a stark contrast to Vancouver's rain-drenched sprawl, its cobblestone streets and Gothic architecture exuding an air of old-world charm. But Aarav wasn't here to admire the scenery. Montreal was Singh's final stronghold in Canada, and the lion was wounded.

The successful raid in Surrey and the capture of Harjeet Kaur and Murshid, a Pawn of ISI had left Singh's network fractured and vulnerable. Yet the mission was far from over. Singh had regrouped with his remaining allies, planning a high-stakes meeting with foreign operatives to finalize a weapons deal. If the intelligence was accurate, the deal would secure Zafar Ali Khan's network access to military-grade equipment, a catastrophic escalation if left unchecked.

Aarav's orders were clear: infiltrate the meeting, gather actionable intelligence, and if possible, dismantle Singh's operation entirely.

That evening, Aarav stood outside a dimly lit warehouse in Montreal's port district, his breath visible in the freezing air. His cover as Arjun Nair remained intact, but Singh's paranoia had grown. Every movement and every interaction would be scrutinized.

Kiara's voice crackled in his earpiece. "Perimeter secure. Singh and his men arrived thirty minutes ago. The foreign buyers are already inside."

"Any sign of backup?" Aarav asked, his eyes scanning the area.

"Negative," Kiara replied. "But don't expect this to be straightforward. Singh's desperate, which makes him dangerous."

Aarav nodded, adjusting his scarf to conceal the discreet microphone clipped to his collar. "Keep the extraction team ready. I'll signal when I'm inside."

The interior of the warehouse was dimly lit, the air thick with the scent of oil and rust. Stacks of crates formed a labyrinth of shadows, and the muffled hum of conversation echoed from the far end of the space. Aarav moved with practiced ease; his footsteps silent as he navigated the narrow pathways.

As he approached the meeting area, he spotted Singh seated at a long table, flanked by two bodyguards. Opposite him were three men in tailored suits, their cold demeanors suggesting military or intelligence backgrounds. A crate beside the table had been pried open, revealing an array of weapons, rifles, grenades, and ammunition.

"Gentlemen," Singh was saying, his voice calm but edged with urgency. "This partnership benefits all of us. My people get the tools they need, and you gain access to a network capable of reaching deep into the heart of India."

One of the buyers, a stern-faced man with a thick Russian accent, replied, "We need guarantees, Mr. Singh. Trust is earned, not given."

Singh leaned back in his chair; his confidence unwavering. "The payment has already been wired. The shipment is ready. All I need is your assurance that this deal remains under the radar, discreet."

Aarav positioned himself behind a stack of crates, his small surveillance camera capturing the scene. Every word and every gesture would be analyzed later, but his immediate priority was to identify the key players and disrupt the deal.

The conversation took a sharp turn when one of Singh's men approached him, whispering something in his ear. Singh's expression darkened, and he stood abruptly.

"Excuse me, gentlemen," he said to the buyers. "I need to deal with a... security matter."

Aarav tensed as Singh and his bodyguards moved toward the rear of the warehouse. He retreated further into the shadows, his hand instinctively reaching for the pistol concealed beneath his coat.

Singh's voice carried through the space. "Arjun Nair. I know you're here."

The words sent a jolt through Aarav, though he remained composed. Singh's tone was measured, but the malice beneath it was unmistakable.

"You've played your part well," Singh continued, his footsteps growing closer. "But did you think you could deceive me?"

Aarav's mind raced. Singh's suspicions had turned into certainty, but how? Had Harjeet Kaur managed to relay something before her capture? Or had Singh simply followed his instincts?

Kiara's voice came through his earpiece. "Aarav, get out now. He knows."

"Not yet," Aarav whispered, his eyes scanning for an escape route.

Singh rounded the corner, his pistol drawn. His bodyguards flanked him, their weapons at the ready. Aarav stepped into view; his pistol raised.

"Mr. Singh," Aarav said evenly. "I suppose this means the trust-building phase is over."

Singh smirked, though his eyes were cold. "Trust is a fragile thing, Mr. Nair. And yours just snapped."

Before Singh could react, Aarav fired a shot, striking the weapon from his hand. The warehouse erupted into chaos as Singh's bodyguards opened fire, the sound of gunshots echoing through the cavernous space.

Aarav dove behind a crate, returning fire with precision. He aimed for the legs and shoulders, incapacitating rather than killing. Singh scrambled for cover, shouting orders to his men.

Kiara's voice crackled in Aarav's earpiece. "Reinforcements inbound. The extraction team is five minutes out."

"Make it three," Aarav replied, his tone clipped.

He moved swiftly through the maze of crates, his sharp instincts guiding him toward the rear exit. Singh was ahead, limping slightly as he tried to escape. Aarav fired a warning shot, forcing Singh to halt.

"It's over, Singh," Aarav said, his voice calm but firm. "Drop the act."

Singh turned slowly; his hands raised. "You have no idea what you're doing," he hissed. "Zafar's reach is far greater than you can imagine."

"I'll take my chances," Aarav replied.

Singh's expression twisted into a sneer. "Even if you stop this deal, the network will survive. You can't kill an idea."

Aarav stepped closer, his pistol trained on Singh. "No, but I can cut off its funding and dismantle its infrastructure. And that starts with you."

Before Singh could respond, the sound of approaching sirens filled the air. , dangerous hawks from R&AW, had arrived to secure the scene and to capture their prey. Singh's buyers scattered, but Aarav knew they wouldn't get far.

As the authorities moved in, Aarav slipped out through the rear exit, blending into the shadows. Back at the safehouse, he uploaded the surveillance footage and debriefed Kiara.

"The deal's been disrupted, and Singh's been captured," Aarav said, his tone measured. "But this isn't the end. Zafar's network is still out there."

Kiara nodded. "One battle at a time. We'll get him."

Aarav stared out the window, his mind already turning to the next phase of the mission. The lion's den had been breached, but the war was far from over.

Chapter 6

The Double Cross

The snow began to fall again as Aarav Menon made his way through the dark alleys of Montreal. The operation had moved swiftly; the capture of Maninder Singh had shaken Zafar Ali Khan's Canadian network, but Aarav knew that the true test was yet to come. Singh was in custody, the weapons shipment had been intercepted, and the ISI operatives were now scattered. But the deeper Aarav dug, the more he realized the mission had become a tangled web of lies, betrayal, and shifting allegiances.

Singh's capture had been too easy, too predictable. Aarav's instincts, honed over years of fieldwork, told him something wasn't right. The deal had gone off without a hitch, but now Singh was talking too much. The information he provided about Zafar's operations in Canada and North America was too detailed and too specific. Was he feeding them lies, or had he been played from the very beginning?

Aarav's thoughts were interrupted by a call. The number was unlisted, but Aarav knew better than to ignore it. He pressed the receiver to his ear.

"It's me," came the voice on the other end. Srinivas Rao.

"Aarav," Srinivas said, his voice tense. "I've just received troubling news. Singh's capture was a setup."

Aarav's heart skipped a beat. "What do you mean, a setup?"

"He gave us too much information too quickly," Srinivas replied. "It's all designed to mislead. Zafar's network in Canada isn't just about arms. There's a larger operation underway, and Singh is playing us."

Aarav swore under his breath. "How do you know this?"

"I've been monitoring his communications," Srinivas said. "Singh's been in contact with someone high up in the Indian government. Someone on the inside."

Aarav's mind raced. If Singh was playing them, that meant there was a mole in their ranks, someone feeding Zafar Ali Khan's network critical intelligence. The implications were staggering.

"How much time do we have?" Aarav asked.

"Not long," Srinivas replied. "I've just received intel that a major operation is set to go live within the next twenty-four hours. You need to find the mole, and you need to do it fast."

The next few hours were a blur of phone calls, encrypted messages, and cold, calculated decisions. Aarav knew that finding the mole was no longer a matter of just tracking down Zafar's network, it was about trust. Who could he trust? His team? His government?

As Aarav and Kiara prepared to launch a covert operation to uncover the mole, he felt the weight of the mission pressing on him. The trail had grown cold, and the risks had never been higher. If he failed now, the consequences would be far-reaching, not just for him but for everyone involved.

The safe house was a dark, sterile room in the heart of Montreal, its walls lined with the hum of computers and satellite feeds. Kiara sat across from Aarav, her eyes scanning the encrypted messages that had just come through. They had traced Singh's movements, piecing together the puzzle of his false confessions. But with every answer, more questions arose.

"Nothing adds up," Kiara said, frustration evident in her voice. "Singh's story about Zafar's network doesn't match the intel we have on the ground. Either he's lying, or someone's been feeding him information to sabotage us."

Aarav stood, his mind racing. He couldn't afford to waste time. The operation that Singh had referenced, the one that would go live in twenty-four hours, was too significant to ignore. Zafar's network was planning something big, something dangerous. And if they didn't stop it now, it could escalate beyond control.

"I'll take point on this," Aarav said, his voice firm. "Kiara, gather everything you can on Singh's contacts. I need to know who's been feeding him this information."

Kiara nodded. "I'll get started. But Aarav... we need to be careful.

Srinivas Rao: The Handler

Srinivas Rao's story begins in the corridors of power, far from the shadowy world of espionage. Born to a family of diplomats, Srinivas ' early years were marked by international exposure. His father, an esteemed Indian Foreign Service officer, was posted in various countries, and Srinivas spent his formative years moving between embassies, living in the rarefied air of diplomatic circles. This unique upbringing gave Srinivas a keen understanding of global politics, power dynamics, and the delicate dance of international relations.

Despite his family's diplomatic pedigree, Srinivas was never content with just observing from the sidelines. He was fascinated by the intricacies of intelligence work, the way secret information could shape the course of nations. After completing his studies in political science at Jawaharlal Nehru University (JNU), where he developed an acute understanding of geopolitical strategies, Srinivas was recruited by R&AW. His smooth demeanor, polished negotiation skills, and a network of contacts built through his diplomatic background made him a valuable asset to the agency.

However, Srinivas 'rise through R&AW was not without challenges. He was a man of ambition, and while his early assignments involved desk jobs and analysis, he longed for something more, something that would place him in the heart of the action. His opportunity came when he was sent undercover to monitor the activities of various terror networks operating in the Middle East. Srinivas' charm and intelligence made him adept at gaining trust, allowing him to infiltrate several extremist factions, but the personal cost was high. Over time, Srinivas found himself caught between the world of statecraft and the morally gray territory of espionage.

It was during a mission in Dubai, where Srinivas was tasked with gaining intelligence on arms trafficking routes, that his worldview began to shift. The information he gathered was valuable, but it came at a personal cost. Srinivas was forced to betray a contact who had once been a friend, a decision that left him questioning his place in the intelligence world. He returned to India more disillusioned, realizing that the world he was operating in was not just about national security, it was about power, manipulation, and a constant struggle for control.

Srinivas 'conflicts were compounded by the growing realization that the boundaries between right and wrong were not always clear. He became more calculating and more willing to make deals with the devil if it meant securing his future in the intelligence community. He began to work not just for the agency, but for himself positioning himself as an unseen power broker in the world of espionage.

His appointment as Aarav's handler in Canada was part of a larger plan. While he presented himself as a loyal and trustworthy superior, Srinivas was secretly maneuvering behind the scenes, gathering intelligence not just for India but for himself. His ultimate goal was to carve out a position of unparalleled influence, using his knowledge of global intelligence networks to play both sides. His loyalty to the agency was fading, replaced by his vision of power, one where he could pull the strings from the shadows and shape the course of global events.

Aarav's search led him back to the core of the operation, to the one place that could hold the answers: the Ministry of Home Affairs in New Delhi. As an intelligence officer, Aarav had access to classified government communications, but he knew that to dig any deeper would risk exposure. He had to tread carefully.

Sitting in front of a computer terminal in the safehouse, Aarav accessed a secure channel that linked him directly to the Ministry's internal server. He scrolled through encrypted messages, intercepted transmissions, and files marked with high-security clearance.

It wasn't long before Aarav found the lead he was looking for: a list of contacts who had met with Maninder Singh in the past few weeks. The names on the list were too familiar.

One name stood out: Colonel Vikram Pratap, a retired officer from the Indian Army with deep ties to the Ministry, now settled in Canada. Aarav knew him from his past work with R&AW, a man who had always been loyal to the nation. Or so Aarav had believed.

The realization hit like a punch to the gut. Colonel Vikram Pratap was the mole.

Aarav's pulse quickened as he read the encrypted messages between Singh and Pratap. The Colonel had been feeding Zafar Ali Khan intelligence on R&AW's operations in Canada, including detailed information on Aarav's movements. Singh's entire capture had been a diversion, orchestrated to buy time and cover up the Colonel's true role in the network.

Aarav slammed his fist against the table, the truth settling like a heavy weight on his chest. His government had been compromised. The mole was someone he had once trusted.

As Aarav relayed the information to Srinivas, his thoughts were a whirlwind. How could he have missed it? How could someone so close to the operation have been feeding Zafar vital intelligence?

"Srinivas, it's Vikram," Aarav said, his voice low with anger. "He's the mole."

There was a brief silence on the other end. "Damn it," Srinivas muttered. "I'll handle it from here. You need to get out of there. The situation just went critical."

"Not yet," Aarav replied, his resolve hardening. "I'm not leaving without Pratap. He's going to pay for this."

Aarav's plan was simple but risky. He needed to confront Colonel Vikram Pratap before the Colonel could alert Zafar's network to the imminent threat. Aarav had learned too much to let this slip away.

He reached out to Kiara, who had tracked Pratap's movements to a remote villa on the outskirts of Montreal. Aarav was familiar with the location. It was a place the Colonel had used as a retreat during his time with R&AW a place no one would think to look.

The villa, located on the outskirts of Montreal, is shrouded in isolation. Tall evergreen trees encircle the property, their snow-laden branches drooping under the weight of winter's grip. The gravel driveway, partially obscured by fresh snowfall, winds toward a two-story structure that is both stately and foreboding.

The villa's stone exterior is weathered but solid, exuding an aura of permanence. The windows are darkened, save for a faint glow emanating from the study. The silence surrounding the property is almost unnatural, broken only by the occasional rustle of the wind or the creak of snow-laden branches swaying in the cold breeze.

Inside, the study is dimly lit, its walls lined with shelves of books and framed military memorabilia. The scent of aged leather and cigar smoke lingers in the air, mixing with the faint metallic tang of whisky from a glass on the desk. A single lamp casts long shadows, accentuating the tension that hangs thick in the room.

The room itself feels like a shrine to Colonel Vikram Pratap's past a place where his loyalty once lay unquestioned but now serves as the setting for Aarav's confrontation with his betrayal.

By the time Aarav reached the villa, night had fallen, casting the landscape into an eerie calm. He crept through the shadows, his movements careful and deliberate. The villa loomed ahead, its windows dark. Aarav approached the front door, his hand steady as he reached for his silenced pistol.

Inside, Pratap sat alone in a dimly lit study, a glass of scotch in hand. The Colonel's expression was unreadable, his posture relaxed, but Aarav could see the tension in his shoulders. He knew that Pratap had to have suspected this moment was coming.

Aarav stepped into the room; his weapon aimed directly at Pratap's chest. "Colonel Vikram Pratap," he said, his voice steady. "You've betrayed everything we stand for."

Pratap didn't flinch. Instead, he set the glass down slowly, his hands raised in mock surrender. "Aarav," he said with a slight chuckle. "You're smarter than this. You know what happens to those who get in too deep."

"Shut up," Aarav snapped. "I don't have time for your games. I'm not here to listen to your excuses."

The confrontation was inevitable. But this time, Aarav wasn't just fighting Zafar's network. He was fighting the betrayal of a man he had once called a colleague, a man who had betrayed everything Aarav believed in. The stakes had never been higher, and this time, the cost was personal.

Aarav and Aanya - "Beneath the Surface"

The air in Aarav's apartment was thick with unspoken tension. The city outside was bathed in the quiet glow of the evening, but inside, everything was alive with quiet urgency. Aarav stood by the window, staring out at the skyline, his mind elsewhere. The weight of his secrets pressed heavily on his chest, and his thoughts were a storm of confusion and longing.

Aanya, sitting silently on the couch, watched him. There was something about him tonight vulnerable, distant, yet at the same time, so undeniably present. She had seen him keep control, always calm and composed, hiding his true emotions behind a professional mask. But tonight, she could feel that mask cracking.

She stood, her steps slow and deliberate, walking toward him. The closer she got, the more she could feel the tension between them, as if the very space they occupied was charged with something neither of them could ignore. She hesitated for a moment, then spoke gently.

"Aarav," her voice was soft but insistent, "What are you holding back?"

He turned to face her, and for the first time in a long while, she saw the conflict in his eyes. The calm, calculating man she had come to know was momentarily lost, replaced by someone much more human. A person carrying the weight of unspoken truths.

"I'm not holding back," he said quietly, his voice barely audible. "I'm trying to protect you, Aanya. From everything I'm involved in."

Aanya's heart quickened at his words. He was afraid of something. Afraid of her, of what she might learn about him. She reached out, her hand brushing lightly against his arm, and for a moment, the world seemed to be still.

"You don't need to protect me, Aarav. I'm not afraid of you." Her voice was calm, but there was an edge of determination in it. "Let me in. Please."

Aarav's breath hitched at her words. He looked down at her hand resting on his arm, and for the first time, he allowed himself to feel the warmth of her touch. Aanya was offering him something he hadn't allowed himself to consider a chance to let go of the walls he had so carefully constructed around himself.

He stepped closer to her, and in that moment, the distance between them, both physical and emotional, disappeared. His lips found hers, but this time, there was no hesitation, no calculation. It was a kiss of release, of surrender. Their bodies seemed to fit together effortlessly as if they had always been meant to be this close.

Aanya's arms wrapped around him, pulling him closer, and deepening the kiss. The world outside the apartment ceased to exist as they stood there, lost in the moment. Every touch, every kiss, was a silent promise, a promise that they would face whatever came their way, together.

Aarav's hands moved slowly over her back, tracing the line of her spine, grounding himself in the presence of someone who truly saw him. The urgency of the moment heightened, but there was also tenderness in every movement as if they were both aware that they were giving each other a piece of their souls.

After a moment, they pulled apart, breathless. Aarav's forehead rested against Aanya's, and for a brief instant, the weight of their world seemed to lift. He closed his eyes, trying to collect his thoughts, but the truth was, he didn't know how to make sense of what was happening between them. All he knew was that, for the first time, he didn't want to pull away.

"Aanya," he whispered, his voice thick with emotion, "I'm not the man you think I am."

"I know," she replied softly, her hand resting gently on his chest. "But right now, I don't need you to be anyone else. I just need you to be here, with me."

Aarav's heart skipped a beat at her words. The vulnerability she showed, the way she was accepting him with all his flaws and secrets, was more than he had ever allowed himself to believe in. But now, at this moment, he knew he didn't want to lose it.

With a quiet but determined breath, he kissed her again. This time, it wasn't about holding back or about fear. It was a kiss of trust, of letting go, and of facing whatever came next together.

Chapter 7

The Enemy Within

The silence between Aarav and Colonel Vikram Pratap was thick, like the air before a storm. Aarav stood motionless, his pistol trained on the man who had once been his mentor, the man who had helped shape his career in R&AW. He had trusted Pratap with his life now, but that trust had turned to ash.

Pratap's expression remained calm, almost detached, as though the confrontation was nothing more than an inconvenience. He leaned back in his chair, the faintest trace of a smile tugging at the corner of his lips.

"Do you think you've won, Aarav?" Pratap said, his voice low and measured. "You're just a cog in a much bigger machine."

Aarav's jaw tightened. He couldn't let the Colonel get under his skin not now. "You've sold out to Zafar," Aarav said coldly. "You betrayed your country. My country. And for what? Money? Power? What's your excuse?"

Pratap's smile faded, replaced by something darker. "It's never been about money, Aarav. You think the world is black and white, that people like me are either good or bad. But there are forces at work here that you'll never understand. You're still too naive."

Aarav's heart pounded in his chest. The anger that had been simmering beneath the surface for days now surged up, threatening to consume him. This man, the one who had guided him through the darkest parts of the intelligence world, was the very reason their operations in Canada had been compromised.

"You're right about one thing," Aarav said, his voice steady, almost dangerously calm. "I may not understand the bigger picture. But I understand betrayal. And I understand that you're not getting away with this."

Pratap's eyes flickered with something close to amusement. "Do you think I'll just let you walk out of here, Aarav? The world you've built for yourself the lies you've told are crumbling around you. And there's nothing you can do to stop it."

Aarav's finger tightened on the trigger, but he didn't pull it. Not yet. Something was unsettling in Pratap's words, something Aarav needed to hear.

"What are you talking about?" Aarav asked, his eyes narrowing.

Pratap leaned forward, his voice dropping to a near whisper. "Zafar isn't the only one playing the game, Aarav. There are others. Powerful people who've been pulling the strings. And you've been their pawn, just like me."

Aarav's pulse quickened. The revelation hit like a slap. Powerful people? Who was Pratap talking about? And what did it mean for the operation?

Before he could respond, Pratap's gaze hardened. "I didn't want this for you, Aarav. You were too good. Too idealistic. You thought you could make a difference. But this game doesn't allow for men like you. We don't allow for men like you to make a difference."

The Vikram Factor

Vikram Pratap was born in the early 1960s in a small town in Haryana to a military family. His father, Major General Harish Pratap, was a decorated officer in the Indian Army, known for his bravery during the 1965 and 1971 wars. Raised with a strong sense of duty and discipline, Vikram followed in his father's footsteps, joining the National Defence Academy (NDA) at the age of 18. He was determined to live up to the legacy of his family and to serve his country with honor.

From the moment he joined the Army, Vikram was marked as a rising star. His intelligence, leadership skills, and fearlessness in the face of danger quickly garnered the attention of his superiors. By the time he was in his mid-thirties, he had already risen to the rank of Lieutenant Colonel, and his career was on the fast track. He was handpicked for special operations, where he would go on to lead several high-profile covert missions in the volatile regions of Jammu and Kashmir, and later, in Afghanistan.

Throughout his career, Vikram remained an idealist, driven by a deep belief in the protection of the nation and the people he served. But that idealism began to erode after a devastating operation in the late 1990s, which saw the loss of several close comrades. The operation, which was meant to infiltrate a terrorist cell in Kashmir, went wrong. Despite careful planning, the mission resulted in the deaths of his team, and the terrorists involved were never apprehended.

In the aftermath, Vikram became disillusioned with the system he had dedicated his life to. He witnessed corruption, political interference in military decisions, and the inability of the higher-ups to protect their men. The bureaucracy within the government made him realize that the missions he was sent on were not always about protecting the nation but about political maneuvering. His trust in the system crumbled, and his sense of duty became clouded by the realization that he was merely a pawn in a much larger game.

Over the next few years, Vikram quietly withdrew from active service and began to entertain alternative ways to make a difference through backdoor channels. He became involved with intelligence operations, initially working for R&AW, but always with a growing sense that he was manipulating events rather than controlling them. His betrayal of India was not one born of greed or ideology but of disillusionment. Vikram had come to believe that the game of espionage was less about serving the nation and more about securing power for those in the shadows. He began to feed sensitive intelligence to enemy forces, positioning himself as a key player in both Indian and foreign intelligence networks.

Aarav's mind raced, a whirlwind of possibilities crashing together. He had thought this mission, this betrayal, was about stopping a terror network. But now, it seems far more complicated. Zafar Ali Khan was a pawn in a much larger game, one that Aarav had been blindly caught up in.

Pratap's words echoed in Aarav's mind: "There are others." Who were these others? And why had he been kept in the dark? The weight of the question gnawed at him. His mission, his entire purpose had been built on a lie.

His eyes never left Pratap, who remained calm, waiting for the next move. Aarav could feel the anger building again, but this time, it was mixed with confusion and a deep sense of betrayal.

"I've spent my entire career fighting for this country," Aarav said, his voice shaking with a mix of fury and disbelief. "And now you're telling me it's all been a game? That I've been playing into someone else's hands?"

Pratap's expression softened, just for a moment. "It was always a game, Aarav. The sooner you accept that, the easier it will be for you."

Aarav's thoughts were interrupted by a sudden noise of footsteps outside the villa. His training kicked in instantly. He motioned for Pratap to stay quiet and crept toward the door, peering out through the small crack.

A small group of armed men had just entered the compound. Aarav recognized them instantly as ISI operatives. The same network that had supported Singh's operations in Canada.

Pratap's voice came from behind him, low and mocking. "You're too late, Aarav. I've already ensured that no one leaves this place alive."

Aarav's mind raced. He needed to act quickly. He couldn't let Pratap's games distract him any longer. Singh's network might be fractured, but there were still powerful players in the shadows, waiting for their moment.

He turned to Pratap, his decision made. "You've sold your soul to the enemy, Vikram. And now, you're going to answer for it."

Before Pratap could react, Aarav fired. The shot struck the Colonel's leg, causing him to collapse with a grunt of pain.

Aarav's earpiece crackled to life. "Aarav, we've got incoming. ISI operatives are moving in from the north. Get out of there, now!"

The urgency in Kiara's voice was unmistakable. Aarav didn't hesitate. He moved quickly, grabbing Pratap by the collar and pulling him toward the exit. The Colonel groaned, but Aarav wasn't interested in hearing his excuses anymore.

Outside, the night had descended into chaos. The ISI operatives were closing in, their weapons raised. Aarav fought to keep his composure, pulling Pratap toward a narrow alley that led toward the extraction point.

The sound of gunfire echoed in the distance. Aarav knew they didn't have much time. He had to neutralize Pratap and ensure the mission was completed no matter the cost.

"Who are these people, Vikram?" Aarav asked, his voice low. "Who's behind this?"

Pratap's lips curled into a bloodied grin. "You'll find out soon enough, Aarav. If you're lucky, you might even survive to see it."

As Aarav dragged the Colonel toward the extraction point, the truth of Pratap's betrayal began to sink in. The operation, the war with Zafar, the alliances he had built all of it had been part of a much larger game. The line between friend and enemy had blurred, and Aarav no longer knew who to trust.

And then, amidst the chaos of the mission, one thought rang clear in Aarav's mind: this was no longer just a battle against terror. This was a war for the very soul of the nation, a fight for survival that would take him into the heart of darkness itself.

Chapter 8

The Storm Breaks

The night air in Montreal was sharp, biting at Aarav Menon's skin as he dashed through the narrow alleyways, his every step echoing in the stillness. The ISI agents were closing in. The walls around him were crumbling, and Aarav could feel the weight of the mission pressing on him. The operation had gone from being about a terrorist network to something much larger, more insidious, an intricate web of betrayal that reached deep into the heart of his government.

Aarav's eyes flicked over to Colonel Vikram Pratap, who lay beside him in the shadows, his leg still bleeding from Aarav's shot. Despite the Colonel's earlier bravado, he now seemed frail, his power and influence no longer the threat they once were.

"You'll never win this, Aarav," Pratap spat out, grimacing in pain. "They'll come for you. They'll come for all of us."

Aarav's face remained impassive as he helped Pratap to his feet, dragging him through the alley. The Colonel had made his choice, and now it was time to deal with the consequences.

"We're already deep in this," Aarav muttered, "and I don't intend to be the one who loses."

Kiara's voice crackled through Aarav's earpiece, cutting through the tension. "Aarav, you've got fifteen minutes before the extraction team arrives. Make it quick."

Aarav nodded. "Understood."

The ISI agents weren't far behind. Aarav could already hear the muffled footsteps in the distance, two agents moving in to surround them. He glanced at Pratap. The Colonel was breathing heavily now, but his defiance was still there, lurking beneath the surface. Aarav's gaze hardened. This man had been a mentor, someone who had once been trusted with the most sensitive operations in R&AW. And now? He was the enemy.

As they reached the extraction point, Aarav's mind raced. He hadn't had time to process everything Pratap had said. The Colonel's words about a larger conspiracy, about powerful people manipulating events from behind the scenes, rang in Aarav's ears. But there was no time to focus on the enormity of it all. The storm was here, and the only way out was forward.

The safe house was a cramped space, one that barely had room for them and the intelligence they had gathered. Aarav set Pratap down on a chair, his eyes flicking over to the computer terminal where Kiara was reviewing the latest data.

The Burn Notice

"We've lost contact with the Indian embassy," Kiara said, her tone urgent. "Aarav, something's off. There's a bigger game going on here. I don't know how deep it goes, but Srinivas ... he's connected to Zafar."

Aarav froze. The name struck him like a blow. Srinivas Rao. His handler. The man who had guided him through every step of this mission, from the moment he had stepped foot in Canada to the successful capture of Singh and the disruption of the weapons deal. How could he be involved with Zafar Ali Khan?

"No," Aarav muttered, shaking his head. "Srinivas 's been clean. He's been the one running the operation, there's no way he's compromised."

Kiara looked at him, her expression grim. "You're missing the bigger picture, Aarav. Srinivas has been feeding us intel, but now it seems like it's been part of a larger strategy, one where we're the pawns."

Aarav's heart pounded in his chest as he replayed the events in his mind. Singh had been too cooperative. The sudden ease with which they had secured their targets. Everything now pointed back to Srinivas. He was the one who had orchestrated their success, but for what purpose?

Kiara's voice broke through his thoughts. "Aarav, I've got something on the network. There's a list of names of people who have been meeting with Zafar and his men, people who have been feeding them information. Srinivas's name is on the list."

Aarav's breath hitched. His mind was a swirl of confusion, disbelief, and fury. How could Srinivas, the man he trusted, be working against him? The implications were staggering. Srinivas wasn't just a mole he was the mastermind. He had been using Aarav and his team as pawns in a much larger game, one that involved more than just arms deals and terror plots.

"Get him on the line," Aarav said, his voice steely with determination. "I want to speak to Srinivas. Now."

Minutes later, Aarav stood alone in the safehouse, staring at the phone as it rang. The silence was deafening, the weight of betrayal pressing down on him. Finally, Srinivas's voice crackled through the speaker, calm as ever.

"Aarav," Srinivas said, his tone laced with amusement, "I'm surprised it took you this long to figure it out."

Aarav's fists clenched. "I should have known. You've been feeding us false intel from the start, haven't you?"

Srinivas chuckled. "False? No. Misleading, yes. But everything I've told you has been part of the plan. You were never meant to win this, Aarav. You were always meant to fall into place, now you are burnt"

Aarav's heart pounded in his chest. "You're working with Zafar."

"I'm working with whoever will ensure the survival of our people," Srinivas replied coldly. "Zafar is just one piece of a much larger puzzle. And now, you're part of that puzzle too."

Aarav could feel the anger bubbling up, threatening to overtake him. "You've been playing me this entire time."

"No, Aarav. I've been guiding you. You just didn't see the game we were playing. You've done your part, now it's time for me to finish mine."

Aarav's hand tightened around the phone. "You've been playing both sides. The truth is, you never wanted to stop Zafar, you wanted to control him."

Srinivas's voice dropped, a touch of bitterness seeping in. "You're learning too late. Do you think Zafar and his network are the problem? You're not seeing the bigger picture. Other players in this game control far more than you or I ever will."

Srinivas had betrayed him. Had used him. And now Aarav had to find a way to turn the tables.

There were too many questions, too many people involved others who had been pulling the strings. But there was one thing Aarav knew for certain: no matter what happened next, he wouldn't let Srinivas win.

The storm was breaking. But Aarav was ready to face it head-on, with every ounce of strength he had left. For now Vikram Prathap was nabbed by R&AW. One more player taken out of the game.

Aarav is back to Montreal for the next challenge.

Chapter 9

The Web Unraveling

The chill of the early morning air cut through Aarav's jacket as he stood on the rooftop of a government building, staring out over the sprawling city of Montreal. Below him, the streets were still waking up people rushing to work, cars honking in the early traffic, but for Aarav, everything had changed. The discovery that Srinivas Rao, the man who had once been his mentor, was at the center of a global espionage network left him grappling with one overwhelming thought: Who else was involved?

The truth had begun to unravel, and Aarav knew that the more he dug, the more tangled the web would become. Srinivas had been just one part of something far larger, powerful figures, within and outside the government, who had manipulated entire operations, feeding information to Zafar Ali Khan and his allies. But who was at the top? And who could he trust?

His thoughts were interrupted by the sharp buzz of his phone. It was Kiara.

"Aarav," she said urgently, "I've been going over Pratap's intel, the documents we seized, everything and there's something you need to see. It's about the network. You need to come to the safehouse, now."

Aarav's heart skipped a beat. What now? He thought. If Kiara was this urgent, it could mean they were on the brink of discovering something crucial.

"I'll be there in ten," he replied, his voice steady despite the rising tension in his chest.

The safe house was located in an inconspicuous residential neighborhood, its modest exterior a far cry from the operations being run inside. As Aarav entered, Kiara was already at the table, surrounded by stacks of files, digital readouts, and encrypted documents. Her expression was grave, a far cry from her usual composed demeanor.

"What have you found?" Aarav asked as he moved to her side.

Kiara pointed to a series of names and dates on her screen. "This," she said, her voice tight with urgency. "I've cross-referenced everything we've seized Pratap's files, Singh's documents, and the communications we intercepted. There's a pattern. A network, hidden in plain sight, operating within the highest echelons of our government."

Aarav leaned in, scanning the screen. The names on the list were unfamiliar to him, high-ranking bureaucrats, military officers, and businessmen, all with connections to Zafar Ali Khan's terror network. But there was one name that made Aarav's stomach churn.

General Arun Malhotra, the head of the Indian Army's Intelligence Directorate.

Aarav's mind raced. The name felt like a betrayal from within the heart of the system he had dedicated his life to protecting. *How deep does this go?* he thought.

"Malhotra?" Aarav asked, his voice steady but his mind a storm of questions. "Are you sure?"

Kiara nodded, her fingers hovering over the screen. "I've confirmed it. Malhotra has been in contact with Zafar's network for years. And I've found the encrypted messages linking him to Srinivas through a private channel only accessible by the highest-level operatives. He's part of the core group pulling the strings, Aarav."

Aarav's world tilted. His first instinct was disbelief, followed quickly by anger. Malhotra? The man who had been entrusted with the security of the nation, a figure whose integrity was unquestioned in R&AW's upper echelons? The man who had mentored generations of operatives and had always been considered untouchable?

"How long has he been involved?" Aarav asked, struggling to keep his voice even.

"For at least the last five years," Kiara replied. "Every operation, every intelligence gathering mission in the last decade has been compromised. Malhotra has been feeding Zafar information, manipulating the flow of intelligence to make sure Zafar's network stays ahead of us. He's been a ghost in the system, pulling strings from within our system and beyond."

Aarav clenched his fists. He knew Malhotra. The general was a man of honor, of discipline. To think that he had been feeding secrets to the enemy for so long was a nightmare come true. And now, Aarav knew the scope of the betrayal: Srinivas had been his conduit, but Malhotra was the mastermind.

"Where do we go from here?" Kiara asked.

Aarav turned to face her, his mind already working through the next steps. "We go after Malhotra. If we can expose him, we'll dismantle this entire network. But we can't do it alone. We need backup someone we can trust."

Kiara nodded. "But we don't have much time, Aarav. Malhotra must know we're on to him by now. He'll be making his move."

The next few hours were a blur of preparations. Aarav and Kiara contacted their trusted assets within R&AW, quietly coordinating a plan to bring Malhotra down. But every move had to be calculated; they had to be certain of their evidence, their next steps. Malhotra was too powerful and too well-connected for them to act without solid proof.

Arun Malhotra was born into a family with a long military legacy. His father, General Raj Malhotra, was a decorated officer who instilled a deep sense of duty, honor, and patriotism in Arun. Growing up, Arun idolized his father and was driven to follow in his footsteps, enrolling in the National Defence Academy (NDA) at a young age. He excelled in his studies and military training, quickly rising through the ranks due to his sharp mind and unwavering commitment.

During his career, Arun became known for his strategic brilliance and unyielding determination in the battlefield.

He participated in several high-profile operations, earning the trust of his superiors and the admiration of his peers. However, despite his success, he always felt like something was missing. The constant sacrifices, the loss of comrades, and the political maneuvering within the higher echelons of the military left a bitter taste in his mouth.

Over time, Arun's faith in the system began to erode. He grew disillusioned with the politics and corruption that often marred decisions, especially during military operations where bureaucratic delays and diplomatic concerns took precedence over national security. The final blow came during a critical operation where, despite his brilliant strategy, the government pulled back due to international pressure. The loss of lives and the failure to achieve the mission left Arun questioning his loyalty to a country that seemed to prioritize diplomacy over action.

It was at this point that Arun encountered the Syndicate, a global, shadowy organization operating in the gray areas of geopolitics and military intelligence. The Syndicate recognized Arun's talents and offered him an alternative a life without the constraints of bureaucracy, where decisions were made by individuals who had the power to act decisively. They promised wealth, influence, and the ability to reshape global power dynamics. The Syndicate also provided him with personal leverage: his family's safety and power that could elevate his position beyond what India could ever offer.

The betrayal began when Arun, feeling trapped by his own idealism and the system's limitations, was offered a deal he couldn't refuse. The Syndicate used his personal frustrations and desires for greater influence as leverage. In exchange for his cooperation, they promised him unprecedented military and political power, while also offering a way to safeguard his family and ensure their continued prosperity.

Initially, Arun justified his actions, telling himself that the Syndicate's goals aligned with his own vision of a better world one where India could rise above the political squabbles that often hindered its progress. But soon, his loyalty shifted, and he became entangled in the Syndicate's dangerous web of operations. He began to feed them critical military intelligence, compromising national security in exchange for personal gain. His strategic insights helped the Syndicate disrupt Indian military operations, destabilize key regions, and further their own global ambitions.

Aarav stared at the map of the city pinned to the wall, tracing the locations of the safehouses, the suspected meeting points, and the military bases. He felt the weight of the operation pressing on him. There were too many unknowns and too many risks. But the moment of truth was coming, and there was no turning back.

"This ends tonight," Aarav muttered to himself, his finger brushing over a spot on the map. He had pinpointed a location a safehouse linked to Malhotra, one that had been under surveillance for weeks.

Kiara was already gathering her gear. "Are you ready?"

Aarav didn't answer immediately. His mind flashed to Srinivas's final words: You've been a pawn. Those words echoed louder with every passing minute. This wasn't just about stopping a terror network anymore. This was about taking down the puppet masters, the people who had been pulling the strings from the shadows.

He turned to Kiara, his expression hardening. "Let's go."

The safe house was just as Aarav had expected: heavily guarded, silent, and foreboding. The night was dark, with only the occasional flicker of streetlights breaking the vast expanse of shadow. Aarav and Kiara moved with precision; their steps quiet as they crept closer to the building's rear entrance.

Aarav's heart beat in his chest, the adrenaline coursing through his veins as they reached the door. He nodded to Kiara, signaling for her to stand by. He moved to the door, his hand on the handle.

This is it, Aarav thought. We either make it out of here alive, or we expose everything.

The door creaked open, and they slipped inside.

The next moments unfolded like a well-rehearsed operation. Guards were neutralized with efficiency, their bodies silent against the cold floor. Inside the safe house, the operation was already underway. Malhotra was meeting with a few of his key allies, the room filled with tension.

Aarav and Kiara quickly surveyed the scene, making sure to remain unseen. Malhotra sat at the head of the table; his face illuminated by the dim light of the overhead lamp. He was discussing something in low tones with a few men, but Aarav could make out the key points for an upcoming attack, the final phase of their operation.

Aarav's pulse quickened. He knew this was their moment. This wasn't just about stopping a terror plot; it was about exposing a conspiracy that ran deeper than he had ever imagined.

"Now," Aarav whispered to Kiara.

They moved with lethal precision, infiltrating the room before Malhotra could react. The general's eyes widened in surprise as he saw Aarav standing there, his gun trained on him.

"You," Malhotra said, his voice low, almost bitter. "I should have known."

Aarav stepped forward, his weapon steady. "This ends tonight, General. You've betrayed everything you were sworn to protect."

The storm had broken, and now, Aarav was finally standing at the center of it. This wasn't just a battle for survival, it was a battle for the future of his country, his agency, and everything he had ever believed in. The web was unraveling, and he was the one who would tear it apart.

Chapter 10

The Heart of Deceit

The tension in the room was palpable, thick as smoke, as Aarav Menon stood face-to-face with General Malhotra, his gun trained on the man who had once been the epitome of loyalty and integrity. The flickering light above cast shadows across the table, where several figures malignant ghosts in this web of deception sat frozen, their expressions a mix of shock and fear.

Aarav's heart pounded in his chest, but his hand was steady. This was the culmination of months of deception, years of work undone by one man's betrayal. He had to see it through. He had to finish what he started.

Malhotra's voice was cold, resigned. "You've already lost, Aarav. Do you think exposing me will stop it all? Do you think you're saving your country? You're too late. The wheels have already been set in motion."

Aarav's gaze never wavered. He had heard it all before these empty words, this twisted justification of betrayal. It was nothing more than a desperate attempt to maintain control. Malhotra had been a part of the conspiracy for years, his hands stained with blood that would never wash clean. But Aarav wasn't going to let him talk his way out of it.

"We're not here for a debate, General," Aarav said, his voice firm. "We're here to end this."

Malhotra's eyes flickered with a moment of fear, perhaps, or the realization that his time was running out. But his defiance remained. "You think you're the first to stand against me? There are others, Aarav. Those who've been with me from the start. You're nothing but a puppet in this game."

Kiara moved quietly behind Aarav; her gun aimed at the men sitting at the table. They didn't dare make a move, their silence deafening. Every step they took, every word they spoke, was calculated. These men were no different from the ones who had betrayed their country before. They had sold their souls to a cause that would burn everything down for power, for control. But tonight, it would be their turn to pay the price.

Aarav's mind was sharp as ever. He couldn't afford to make a mistake. He'd come this far, but the mission was far from over. Zafar's network, and the forces that supported it, had to be dismantled. Malhotra was just the beginning.

"You want me to explain, Aarav? Fine. Let me enlighten you," Malhotra continued, his voice laced with bitter arrogance. "Zafar is nothing. A puppet, just like you. There are those behind him far more dangerous than anything you've ever faced. They are the ones who control the game. The ones who decide who lives, who dies."

Aarav narrowed his eyes. This was the moment he had feared. The realization that Zafar was only one part of a much larger, more insidious network.

Malhotra leaned back in his chair, a look of grim satisfaction on his face. "You've been chasing shadows, Aarav. Chasing me. You don't even know who's pulling the strings."

Kiara took a step forward, her voice cutting through the tension. "Who? Who's behind all of this, Malhotra?"

Malhotra smiled, but it was a smile tinged with finality. "You'll never find them. Not in time. The country is already at war, Aarav. And you well, you're just too late to do anything about it."

The words hung in the air like a death sentence. Aarav's mind raced. Malhotra was right about one thing: this conspiracy was bigger than he had imagined. It wasn't just Zafar; it wasn't just a network of extremists there were others. People with more power, have more influence. The type of people who could make decisions on a scale that Aarav couldn't even fathom.

But that didn't matter. Not now. Not while Malhotra was sitting there, defiant, convinced he had already won.

Aarav's grip on his weapon tightened. "The game ends tonight, Malhotra," he said quietly, his voice a lethal whisper. "You were right about one thing, though. I'm too late... to stop you. But I'm not too late to make sure you never see the light of day again."

The tension broke like a snapped wire. In a single fluid motion, Aarav pulled the trigger. The sound of the gunshot reverberated through the room, the report loud and final. Malhotra's body jerked as the bullet struck, his expression frozen in shock. His eyes flickered one last time, a look of disbelief in them before the general slumped forward, lifeless.

Kiara was already moving, ensuring the other men at the table were subdued. But Aarav didn't take his eyes off the general's body. He had expected anger, a rush of adrenaline. But instead, there was only a deep, hollow feeling. The mission was done, but the price had been paid long before tonight.

The storm hadn't just broken, it had torn apart everything Aarav had believed in. The people he had trusted, the system he had been a part of, were all built on lies. And now, those lies have come to light.

"Aarav," Kiara's voice broke through his thoughts. "We've got a problem."

Aarav snapped out of his trance, turning to face her. The calm in her eyes was replaced by a look of grim urgency.

"What is it?" Aarav asked, his voice steady but his mind still reeling.

"We've received an encrypted transmission," Kiara said. "From Malhotra's contact. The operation isn't over. There's a bigger play at work."

Aarav's pulse quickened as Kiara handed him a tablet with the transmission. The message was short, but its implications were massive:

"The storm is only the beginning. Act quickly. The 'Syndicate' is already mobilizing. Prepare for the fallout. Everything you've uncovered is nothing compared to what's coming. Prepare for war."

The message was a warning one that sent a cold shiver through Aarav's spine. The conspiracy wasn't just a national issue. It was global. And someone, somewhere, was orchestrating a new phase of the game.

"Aarav, what do we do now?" Kiara asked her voice tight with urgency.

Aarav turned to her; his mind now focused. They weren't done. Far from it. They had exposed one layer of the conspiracy, but this was just the beginning.

"We prepare for war," Aarav said, his voice firm, resolute. "We take the fight to them. Whoever 'the syndicate' is, they'll know we're coming."

As they prepared for the next phase of the operation, Aarav's thoughts returned to the message. The others. There were more players in this game more people who had been orchestrating the chaos from the shadows. But now, Aarav was no longer playing their game. He would make his own rules.

And this time, he wouldn't stop until he had dismantled their entire operation, piece by piece.

Chapter 11

The Silent War

The air in Montreal felt heavy, as though the weight of impending conflict was pressing down on everything. For the first time, Aarav Menon felt as though he was no longer in control of the situation. His entire world, once grounded in the pursuit of justice and national security, had been flipped upside down by the revelation that a shadowy, far-reaching conspiracy had taken root within the heart of his government. The operation that had started with the simple goal of thwarting a terror network was now a battle against something far more insidious: an international web of power and corruption, with threads leading to the highest echelons of authority.

Aarav's mind raced. The encrypted message had made it clear: Malhotra's death wasn't the end. It was only the beginning of a much larger conflict. The people behind Zafar's network, the "others" referred to in the message, were mobilizing. Whoever they were, they had the resources, the influence, and the secrecy to carry out an operation that could shake the foundations of global security.

"Aarav," Kiara's voice broke through his thoughts, steady but tense. "We've got confirmation. The transmission wasn't a bluff. There's a major operation in motion. It's happening now, across multiple cities."

Aarav turned to face her; his jaw clenched. "What are they targeting?"

"Military installations," Kiara replied, her fingers flying over the screen as she scrolled through the intel. "Strategic points. International communications hubs. They're trying to cripple the global intelligence network."

Aarav's stomach tightened. The scale of the operation was staggering. If they succeeded, it would be a blow to the very core of international security. Governments would fall. Alliances would crumble. The world would be plunged into chaos.

"We need to act fast," Aarav said, his voice cold with determination. "We can't let this go through unchecked. We need to find where they're striking next, and we need to stop them before they set everything in motion."

The next few hours passed in a blur of activity. Aarav and Kiara combed through the intel, narrowing down possible locations where the "syndicate" might strike next. Their efforts were hindered by the fragmented nature of the operation; each attack was being orchestrated by different factions, but all were tied to the same network. They were up against an enemy that knew how to cover its tracks, and that had infiltrated every layer of government and military communication.

"We've identified a possible target," Kiara said, her face illuminated by the glow of the screen. "A satellite communications facility in the Arctic Circle. If they control that, they'll have access to real-time global communications. That's where they'll launch the next phase of their attack."

Aarav's heart skipped a beat. This was the moment when everything would either fall apart or be held together. If they lost the satellite facility, the consequences would be catastrophic. "Get me the coordinates. We're going there."

The journey to the Arctic Circle was long, the journey itself as cold and isolating as the mission ahead. Aarav's mind raced with plans, contingencies, and anything he could use to get ahead of the enemy. But every step he took seemed to lead him further into the unknown. His every move, every decision, felt like it was being watched by unseen eyes.

Kiara had already begun preparing the infiltration plan for the facility. The satellite communications station was heavily guarded, a remote outpost that had been established as a joint effort between several nations. Its isolation, combined with its critical importance, made it a prime target.

The Arctic Circle is a world of extremes. The snow stretches endlessly in all directions, a blinding white expanse broken only by jagged icebergs and the occasional mountain ridge. The wind howls relentlessly, cutting through layers of clothing like a blade. The air is crisp and bitter, filled with the scent of ice and frost.

In the endless twilight, the sun never truly rises, casting a dim, ethereal glow across the icy landscape. The stillness of the land is punctuated only by the occasional crack of shifting ice, a reminder of the violent forces at play beneath the surface. Every step through the snow is a battle against nature, each breath a struggle against the bitter cold.

They arrived at the perimeter under the cover of darkness. The snow-covered landscape stretched out in all directions, a white void that seemed to swallow every sound. The temperature was freezing, but Aarav barely noticed it. The cold had become a part of him, something that reminded him of how small they were in the grand scheme of things, how vulnerable, despite their preparation.

"This is it," Kiara whispered, her eyes scanning the facility ahead. "There's no turning back now. If we go in, we do it fast."

Aarav nodded, steeling himself for what lay ahead. The enemy was inside, waiting to carry out their operation. They had to stop it, or else the consequences would be far greater than any of them could predict.

Inside the facility, the tension was thick. The enemy knew they were coming. Aarav and Kiara were certain of it. The facility's security had been ramped up in the past few days, its perimeter fortified. But Aarav had prepared for this. He had anticipated every move, every contingency.

They slipped past the outer security, their movements quick and calculated. The facility was eerily silent, save for the soft hum of machinery and the occasional buzz of communication equipment. The deeper they moved into the facility, the more urgent their mission became. The clock was ticking, and they had to find the command center.

Aarav turned to Kiara, his voice barely above a whisper. "We get to the communications room. Shut down their access. We can't let them send out the signal."

Kiara nodded; her eyes sharp as ever. "On it."

They moved swiftly, bypassing guards with silent efficiency. Aarav's senses were heightened, his focus absolute. He could feel the weight of the mission pressing on him. This wasn't just about stopping an attack it was about preventing the world from descending into chaos.

They reached the communications hub, a room at the heart of the facility. Aarav motioned for Kiara to cover him as he approached the door. The lock clicked open with a soft turn of the handle, and they slipped inside.

The room was filled with rows of computers, glowing screens displaying real-time satellite data. At the far end of the room, several operatives sat, their focus entirely on the work before them. They hadn't noticed Aarav and Kiara's presence.

Aarav didn't hesitate. He moved swiftly, taking out the nearest operative with a single, clean shot. The other operatives scrambled, but Kiara was already on them, her rifle trained on the next target. The room erupted into chaos as Aarav made his way to the control console.

He typed quickly, his fingers flying over the keys. The screens in front of him flickered, then went black. He was in.

"We've lost access to the communications grid," Aarav said, his voice cold. "They won't be able to send out the signal now."

The operatives who had been guarding the room made a last-ditch effort to stop them, but it was too late. Kiara's rifle rang out, and the last of the attackers fell to the ground.

Aarav's mind was already moving to the next step. "We need to shut this place down completely," he said. "Get to the backup systems. We can't leave anything behind."

Kiara nodded, following him as they moved through the facility's corridors. The network was broken for now, but they had to ensure that no part of the operation remained intact.

As they reached the backup systems, Aarav's mind flashed back to the encrypted message that had led them here. The "others" were still out there planning. And the clock was ticking down faster than he could keep up.

In the final moments of the mission, as the systems were destroyed and the facility was rendered useless, Aarav stood still for a moment, staring out across the vast, empty expanse of snow. The storm had broken, but the world was far from safe.

The fight was far from over.

Chapter 12

The Silent Echo

The hum of the destroyed communications facility slowly faded behind them as Aarav and Kiara made their way back to the extraction point. The night air was bitterly cold, biting through their gear, but neither of them felt it. Their minds were consumed by the events that had unfolded the knowledge that they had just disrupted a larger operation, one with global implications, but the cold realization that this was only one small victory in a far bigger war.

Aarav's mind raced as they moved through the snow, the weight of everything he had uncovered pressing down on him. The operation in the Arctic Circle had been a success in one sense. They had prevented the enemy from gaining control of the satellite communications hub, but that wasn't the end of it. The encrypted messages, the talk of the "syndicate," had confirmed what Aarav had feared: there was an international faction behind the chaos, a hidden group manipulating global conflicts for reasons Aarav couldn't yet fully comprehend.

His mind kept returning to the words Malhotra had said just before his death You've been chasing shadows, Aarav. The others are already mobilizing. It was clear now: Zafar was only a pawn, and Malhotra had been playing a much larger game. But who were these others? And why hadn't Aarav and his team known about them until now?

"What now?" Kiara asked, breaking the silence as they reached the rendezvous point. The extraction team was already waiting, the black SUV's engine running in the cold.

Aarav didn't answer immediately. He knew what had to be done, but it felt like they were standing at the edge of a cliff, waiting for the inevitable. They had disrupted the operation at the communications facility, but the network was still out there, still moving in the shadows. And Srinivas, his former mentor, was still a ghost haunting their every step.

"I don't know yet," Aarav replied quietly. "But we have to get back to R&AW. We need to piece this together before they make their next move. If Malhotra was part of it, if Srinivas is involved… we're still missing a key part of the puzzle."

Back at the safehouse, Kiara immediately started working on decrypting the new intel they had gathered, while Aarav paced the room. The storm outside had intensified, the wind howling against the windows. It was a fitting metaphor for the chaos they were now embroiled in. Aarav had known espionage was a dangerous game, but this felt different. The players involved were far bigger than he had imagined.

Aarav sat down in front of his laptop, flipping through the documents they had retrieved from the Arctic facility. The encrypted files contained information about the communications hub and several high-level meetings between international operatives, but most of it was still indecipherable.

Kiara worked silently next to him; her face illuminated by the screen. "Aarav," she said after a few minutes, "I think I've found something."

Aarav turned to her, his eyes narrowing. "What is it?"

Kiara's fingers danced across the keyboard. "There's a name. It keeps coming up in the communications between Zafar's network and Malhotra's people. Samir Ahmed. He's been coordinating operations between North America, Europe, and the Middle East. His role is key to everything."

Aarav's eyes flickered with recognition. Samir Ahmed. He had heard the name before an enigmatic figure who was rumored to have connections in multiple countries, with ties to both extremist factions and government officials. A shadow broker, pulling strings from the darkness.

Kiara paused for a moment. "He's not just a broker. He's been working with people in intelligence agencies, government agencies, and militaries across the globe. This goes beyond Zafar. It's much larger."

Aarav rubbed his temples, the weight of the situation sinking in. "How do we find him?"

Kiara turned the screen toward Aarav, showing a series of encrypted communications.

"We track his money. His transactions have been routed through multiple accounts across the globe. If we can follow the money, we might be able to get to him."

The next few hours were a blur of activity. Aarav and Kiara worked tirelessly, following leads, decrypting files, and piecing together the puzzle. But the more they uncovered, the clearer it became that Samir Ahmed wasn't just another terrorist mastermind. He was the linchpin in a global operation that spanned continents, with connections to some of the most powerful and dangerous figures in the world. The implications were staggering.

Finally, after what felt like an eternity, Kiara looked up from her screen. "I've got something," she said, her voice tense. "I found a direct link to one of his assets in the Middle East, someone named Farouk Al-Sayyid. If we can track him down, we might get closer to Ahmed."

Aarav stood up abruptly, his mind clicking into gear. This was it. The breakthrough they needed. "Where is he?"

Kiara's fingers flew across the keyboard. "He's scheduled to meet with one of the others, a high-level operative in Cairo. If we intercept that meeting, we can take him down and get the intel we need to get to Samir Ahmed."

Hours later, Aarav and Kiara were en route to Cairo. The mission was taking shape now, the pieces of the puzzle falling into place. They would intercept Farouk Al-Sayyid's meeting, and from there, they would gain access to the heart of the operation, the mastermind behind the global conspiracy. The network was large, yes, but it wasn't impenetrable.

Aarav looked out the window as the plane descended into Cairo, his mind focused on the task ahead. The storm hadn't just broken, it had torn everything apart. And now, he was going after the men who had set it all in motion.

Cairo, with its blend of ancient mystique and modern chaos, is alive with sound and color. The air is thick, carrying the scent of spices and street food from the bustling market squares. The sun beats down on the stone buildings, casting long, sharp shadows that stretch across the city's labyrinthine streets. The call to prayer echoes from the towering minarets, weaving through the cacophony of honking cars and the murmurs of vendors haggling in the souks.

The Nile, winding through the city, reflects the golden hues of the setting sun, its calm surface contrasting with the relentless energy of the streets. The city feels both timeless and on the edge of a new era, with the Great Pyramids looming in the distance, ancient structures that bear silent witness to the changing world around them.

The night in Cairo was thick with humidity, the air heavy with the scent of sand and dust. Aarav and Kiara moved swiftly through the crowded streets, keeping to the shadows as they approached the location of the meeting. They had received word that Farouk Al-Sayyid was meeting with a high-ranking member of an international syndicate, a group that was allegedly responsible for coordinating several covert operations across the Middle East.

The rendezvous point was an old, abandoned building on the outskirts of the city, an ideal location for a covert exchange. Aarav's instincts were sharp, every nerve on edge. They were close now, so close to uncovering the truth behind everything.

Aarav signaled for Kiara to stay low as they approached the building, their steps synchronized. The night felt suffocating, every sound amplified in the stillness. They crept around the back of the building, finding a vantage point where they could watch the meeting unfold without being seen.

"Farouk's inside," Kiara whispered. "We can take him out, but we need to be careful. We don't know who he's meeting with."

Aarav nodded. "We do this fast. No mistakes."

Inside, the room was dimly lit, with shadows playing along the cracked walls. Farouk Al-Sayyid sat at a table, his back to the door. Aarav and Kiara moved in quickly, silently, their movements fluid and precise. They were almost there when the door opened, and a tall figure stepped inside, his silhouette casting a long shadow across the room.

Aarav's pulse quickened. This wasn't just a meeting; it was a trap. The figure who had just entered was Samir Ahmed himself. The man who had been orchestrating the entire operation. The mastermind.

The game had changed.

Chapter 13

The Mastermind Revealed

The air in the abandoned building seemed to grow thicker as if the very walls were closing in on Aarav and Kiara. The dim light from a single hanging bulb illuminated Farouk Al-Sayyid, who sat hunched at the table, his face shadowed. But it was the man standing just inside the door, the figure emerging from the darkness, that sent a ripple of unease down Aarav's spine.

Samir Ahmed. The man who had remained a ghost in the system, the one pulling the strings from behind the scenes. Aarav had known this day would come, but facing the architect of the entire operation was different than he had imagined. This wasn't just another adversary. This was the culmination of everything that had shattered his world, the reason why Zafar's network had grown so powerful, and why his government had been compromised.

Aarav didn't flinch. He kept his gun steady, his eyes locked on Samir. Kiara's presence beside him was a silent reassurance, but she, too, was watching the scene unfold with the same intensity.

Samir stepped into the room with the deliberate pace of a man who knew he was in control. His dark eyes swept over Farouk, then flicked toward Aarav, a small smile tugging at the corner of his lips.

"So, this is the man who's been causing all the trouble," Samir said in a smooth, measured voice, his accent unmistakably European. "Aarav Menon. You've been quite the thorn in my side."

Aarav's pulse quickened, but he didn't let it show. "I'm here to stop you, Ahmed. All of this ends tonight."

Samir's smile widened, but there was no warmth in it. "You think you can stop me?" he asked, his voice dripping with amusement. "I've been preparing for this moment for years. You're a small piece in a much larger game, Aarav. But then, you always were just a pawn."

The words hit like a slap, but Aarav kept his focus. He couldn't afford to lose control now. Everything had led up to this moment, and he knew that whatever Samir said or did, he had to be the one to end it.

"You're wrong, Samir," Aarav replied, his voice steady. "I've learned more than you think. And I'm not the pawn anymore."

Samir chuckled softly; the sound almost mocking. "You were the pawn. But you've never realized that the game is already over, have you? I've won. You've walked right into my trap."

Before Aarav could respond, Samir's hand moved swiftly, pulling something from his jacket. A small device, sleek and black, glinted in the low light. Aarav's instincts flared. He recognized the device instantly as a detonation trigger. Samir wasn't just here to talk. He had set up a final, deadly gambit.

Aarav's heart skipped a beat. "What have you done?"

Samir's smile grew wider, a dangerous gleam in his eyes. "This building is rigged with explosives. I knew you would come. You're predictable, Aarav. Your sense of justice, your need to do the right thing, it's what makes you so easy to manipulate."

Kiara's eyes flicked to the device in Samir's hand, and her voice was low but urgent. "How many are there? How much time?"

Samir shrugged casually. "Not much. Just enough to make sure you understand how small you are. Five minutes, maybe. And then this entire building along with any evidence you might have gathered will disappear into the night."

Aarav's mind raced. They had to stop him. They had to stop the trigger from going off. But Samir wasn't just holding a detonator, he was holding the key to everything. He was the mastermind who had pulled every string and played every game. And now he was making his move.

"Where's Srinivas?" Aarav asked, his voice steady but edged with suspicion. "You think you've won, but Srinivas, he's been working for you all along. Where is he now?"

Samir's eyes flickered with a hint of annoyance, perhaps but he quickly masked it with a forced smile. "Srinivas was a tool. He was useful for a time, but like all tools, he was discarded when he outlived his purpose. Don't waste your time thinking about him."

Aarav felt a pang of anger. Srinivas had been his mentor, his friend. To hear Samir speak of him like that, as though he was nothing more than a disposable asset it was almost too much to bear. But Aarav couldn't afford to let emotion cloud his judgment.

"We're not leaving here until you explain everything," Aarav said, stepping closer, his gun still trained on Samir. "You've been orchestrating this entire thing: the bombs, the global chaos, the manipulation of governments. What's your endgame?"

Samir's smile softened as if Aarav had just asked a question he had been waiting for. "Endgame? There is no endgame. This is only the beginning, Aarav. I've planned for every possibility, every contingency. You think you can stop me, but you can't. This war is bigger than anything you or your agency could ever imagine. The world as you know it is on the brink of collapse. And I, I will be the one to ensure that it rises anew under my control."

Aarav clenched his jaw. "You're delusional."

Samir raised his eyebrows, unperturbed by the accusation. "Am I? Or am I simply more aware of the way the world works? You see, Aarav, the idea of order is just an illusion. There is no true stability. What I'm doing is creating a new order, a new way of life, where the ones who control power control the world. It's inevitable. You can't fight it."

Aarav shook his head, his voice low and filled with resolve. "You're wrong. People like you always think they're in control. But there's always someone who comes to tear it all down."

A sudden burst of gunfire interrupted their conversation. Farouk Al-Sayyid had made a move. His gun was aimed at Aarav, but before he could pull the trigger, Kiara's shot rang out, striking him in the chest. Farouk fell to the ground, lifeless.

Aarav's heart pounded. They didn't have much time. If Samir had truly rigged the building, they needed to act fast.

Samir's eyes narrowed, but there was no fear, only a steely determination. "You'll regret this, Aarav. You can't stop what's already in motion. This is bigger than you'll ever understand."

Aarav took a step forward, his gun still aimed at Samir. "I've already stopped you. The game ends here."

But Samir wasn't finished yet. He reached into his coat pocket, pulling out another device. This one was different. Aarav's heart skipped a beat as he recognized it as a keycard. He held it up in front of Aarav, his smile returning.

"You think you can stop the bombs?" Samir sneered. "This keycard is the master code. You'll never disarm them without it."

Aarav's mind raced. Samir had thought of everything. There was no way to win unless…

In a flash, Aarav lunged forward, closing the distance between them. Samir didn't see it coming. Aarav knocked the keycard from his hand, sending it skittering across the floor. But before he could secure it, Samir was already reaching for a second device, this one far more dangerous.

"Aarav, get back!" Kiara shouted; her voice tinged with urgency.

But it was too late. The explosion shook the building to its core.

The world erupted around them. The walls cracked, debris fell from the ceiling, and the ground beneath them shook violently. Aarav's ears rang with the deafening sound of the explosion, his body slammed against the floor.

Amid the chaos, he managed to look up, seeing Samir standing there, unscathed. The man was a specter, a phantom. The explosion had been a diversion, a way to escape.

Aarav pushed himself to his feet, but Kiara was already moving. "We need to get out of here. Now!" she shouted.

They made their way toward the exit, the building groaning and cracking around them. As Aarav glanced back one last time, he saw the silhouette of Samir disappearing into the shadows. The mastermind had slipped away once again.

But Aarav knew one thing for certain: this war was far from over. The storm was still raging, and no matter what, he wouldn't stop until he had dismantled it, piece by piece.

Chapter 14

The Calm Before the Storm

The escape from the collapsing building was a blur of action and instinct. Aarav and Kiara sprinted through the crumbling corridors, the walls shaking with each aftershock from the explosion. Debris and dust filled the air, but they pushed forward, their training kicking in as they weaved through the wreckage. The facility was coming apart at the seams, the detonation only a small part of the broader, catastrophic plan Samir Ahmed had put into motion.

They reached the exit, the bitterly cold night air a stark contrast to the inferno they had just escaped. The streets outside were deserted, but the sounds of approaching sirens told them they didn't have much time. They needed to get out of there, regroup, and plan their next move.

"Kiara," Aarav said, breathless as they jogged toward the extraction vehicle parked several blocks away, "we can't keep running from him. Samir is still out there. He's too powerful."

Kiara nodded; her face set in grim determination. "I know. But we need to go back to the agency. We need to get intel and make contact with our allies. The world is shifting, Aarav. We can't do this alone."

As they reached the car, Aarav couldn't shake the feeling of being one step behind, of knowing that every move he made was being watched, calculated. Samir had orchestrated this entire operation, and now he was slipping through their fingers once again. Aarav's mind raced with possibilities, trying to anticipate where the enemy would strike next. But no matter how many angles he considered, the game was changing. The stakes were higher than ever.

Back at the safehouse, Kiara immediately got to work on pulling together what little intel they had gathered. The explosion at the communications facility had been a setback, but it had also given them a glimpse into Samir's true power. His network wasn't just a terror operation it was an international web, a clandestine operation that spanned continents and governments. This was bigger than anything Aarav had ever encountered, and it was clear that whoever was behind it had the resources to ensure their plans went undetected.

Aarav sat in silence, staring at the map spread out before him. The pieces were scattered, but they weren't connecting. What was Samir's ultimate goal? And more importantly, who was helping him? The "others" Samir had mentioned as the ones who controlled the game from the shadows remained a mystery. But Aarav knew one thing: they were out there, and they were preparing for something much larger.

Kiara's voice broke through his thoughts. "Aarav, I've been running some cross-checks. The encrypted data from the facility... it's pointing to another location."

Aarav snapped to attention, his pulse quickening. "Where?"

Kiara's fingers hovered over the keyboard. "A secure compound in Switzerland. It's isolated, but it has connections to several international banking operations. And I found a link to a meeting scheduled for tomorrow."

Aarav leaned forward, his mind already racing through the possibilities. "Samir is making his move. If we can intercept that meeting, we might be able to find out who he's working with."

The flight to Switzerland was long, but it gave Aarav the time he needed to think. He had already come to terms with the fact that this mission wasn't going to end easily. They were chasing ghosts, and the more they uncovered, the less certain they were of who the real enemy was. But one thing was clear: Samir was the key. He was the one orchestrating everything, and if Aarav could get to him, he could dismantle the entire operation.

But as they neared the compound, Aarav's gut told him something wasn't right. The air had changed, and the tension in the mission was now palpable. Samir's network wasn't just a loose group of radicals, it was a highly organized operation that was prepared to go to any lengths to ensure its survival.

"Aarav," Kiara said, her voice sharp with concern, "I've been reviewing the intel. This compound is heavily guarded. It's not just a meeting. We're dealing with high-profile targets here. This could be their headquarters."

Aarav nodded, his mind already working through the plan. "We move in quietly, gather intel, and get out before they realize we're there. We can't afford another misstep."

They arrived at the compound in the dead of night, the moonlight casting eerie shadows across the walls of the secluded villa. The exterior was almost impossibly perfect, with no sign of surveillance, and no guards in sight. But Aarav knew better than to trust appearances.

"We'll enter through the eastern perimeter," Aarav said quietly. "Stay sharp. We're not just hunting for information anymore. We're hunting the heart of this operation."

As they moved through the compound, Aarav's senses were on high alert. The building's interior was just as pristine as the exterior, with white walls and spotless floors. But it felt wrong, too perfect, like it had been designed to deceive. They reached the inner chambers quickly, bypassing security with ease. Inside, the tech was impressive sophisticated encryption, communications equipment, and high-level surveillance systems.

"Do you hear that?" Kiara whispered, her voice tense.

Aarav paused, his breath shallow. From behind the closed door ahead, he could hear muffled voices, a conversation in progress. He motioned for Kiara to stay low, and they approached the door, their hearts pounding in sync.

Inside, they saw figures gathered around a table, a heated discussion unfolding in low tones. At the center of the group was Samir, his back to them, speaking to several men in military garb and suits.

"This operation is more than just a political maneuver," Samir said, his voice smooth but filled with authority. "We control the narrative now. The world's leaders are already positioning themselves. It's time for the final phase. When the time comes, we'll strike swiftly, decisively. The governments will crumble, and we'll be the ones holding the strings."

The words hit Aarav like a punch to the gut. This wasn't just a terror plot. This was a carefully orchestrated plan to dismantle the world order. And Samir was at the center of it.

Aarav's grip tightened on his weapon. This was it. The final confrontation. The fate of everything he had worked for was hanging by a thread.

"Move in," Aarav whispered to Kiara.

They stormed into the room, weapons drawn. Samir turned slowly, his expression betraying no surprise.

"Did you think you could stop me?" Samir asked, his voice eerily calm. "You've already lost."

Before Aarav could respond, the doors burst open, and armed guards flooded into the room, weapons raised. The mission was slipping through their fingers once again. But Aarav wasn't backing down.

He was going to make sure this ended tonight.

Chapter 15

The Master's Game

The building seemed to pulse with the intensity of the moment. Every footstep echoed in the narrow hallways; the sound amplified by the tension in the air. Aarav's heart hammered in his chest as he moved with Kiara through the compound. The situation had escalated beyond anything he could have prepared for. Samir Ahmed, the elusive mastermind behind the chaos, was no longer a phantom. He was standing right in front of them, orchestrating everything from behind the scenes, and now, everything was falling into place.

The atmosphere inside the room was thick with anticipation. Samir stood in the center, calm and collected, as guards rushed toward them. Aarav's eyes locked onto him. He wasn't just an enemy, he was the man who had been pulling the strings from the shadows, setting events in motion, and manipulating everyone around him.

"You think you can stop me, Aarav?" Samir's voice was smooth, almost mocking, as he faced them with a cold smile. "You've been playing right into my hands."

Aarav didn't flinch, keeping his focus on the enemy in front of him. "I'm not here to talk, Samir. I'm here to end this."

The room erupted into action. Aarav and Kiara moved swiftly, eliminating guards with precise shots. The facility's defenses crumbled around them, but Samir remained calm, his confidence unshaken.

"You've only scratched the surface," Samir said, almost with amusement, as he stepped back from the chaos unfolding. "This is only the beginning. Do you think you can stop what's already in motion? You've lost, Aarav. The world is on the brink of change. A change I'll control."

Aarav's anger flared, but he forced himself to stay composed. "I'm not here to hear your delusions. I'm here to take you down."

As they moved deeper into the compound, the situation became more urgent. Kiara provided cover while Aarav advanced, each step bringing them closer to the heart of the operation. The walls around them seemed to pulse with the weight of everything that had led them here: the global manipulation, the deception, and the intricate web of lies that Samir had carefully woven.

"You've been chasing shadows," Samir's voice echoed through the hallways as Aarav approached. "But you'll never find the truth. I control everything now. Your efforts were futile."

Aarav's grip tightened on his weapon as the final confrontation loomed. They were on the verge of uncovering the truth, but Samir wasn't going down without a fight. The room ahead was filled with tense silence, and Aarav knew this was where the battle would be decided.

They reached the core of the facility, and Samir was waiting. But now, something felt different. The air was thick with the realization that Samir had known they were coming. His calmness, and his presence, made it clear that he was in control. He wasn't worried. He had planned for everything.

"You're too late, Aarav," Samir said, as he stepped forward, eyes cold and calculating. "Everything has already been set in motion. The operation is unstoppable. You're just a small part of a much larger plan, one that you can't even begin to comprehend."

Aarav stared at him down, his resolve unwavering. "I'm not here to understand you, Samir. I'm here to stop you."

Samir's smile faded slightly. "You still don't understand. You've been fighting for a system that is already crumbling. I'm not the cause of the chaos. I'm the solution. And once I'm done, the world will be mine to rebuild."

Before Aarav could respond, an explosion rocked the building. The force of the blast sent them both reeling, but Samir remained unshaken.

Aarav pushed himself up from the debris, his vision blurred from the explosion. The smoke was thick, but he could see Samir standing unharmed, a wry smile on his face. It was a chilling sight. The man was confident, almost pleased with the destruction.

"Did you think you could stop me with brute force?" Samir asked, almost pityingly. "You're too late. The networks are already in place. The final phase is already underway. The governments are falling, and soon, the world will be as I've always envisioned it."

Aarav clenched his jaw. He wasn't here for words anymore. The game was over. They were running out of time, and Samir had made his move. But this wasn't the end. Not yet.

"You're wrong, Samir," Aarav said, his voice cold and full of resolve. "You think you've won. But the world you're building will never stand. It will fall, just like every empire before it. You can't control everything."

Samir's eyes gleamed with something dark, something far more dangerous than Aarav had anticipated. "We'll see about that, won't we?"

Kiara's voice broke through the tension. "Aarav, we have to move now!"

Aarav's pulse quickened as he turned to Kiara, realizing just how much time they had lost. The walls of the facility were closing in, and the stakes had never been higher. "We need to end this now," Aarav said, his voice firm, as he charged toward Samir, determined to put an end to the madness.

At that moment, everything blurred. Aarav and Samir collided a showdown that had been inevitable from the start. The fight was fierce, each one of them determined to claim victory. But in the end, only one of them could walk away.

As the dust settled, Aarav stood over the remnants of the compound, his breath heavy, his body bruised, but his spirit unbroken. Samir was gone, and the threat had been neutralized for now.

But the war was far from over. There were others out there, others who had been watching from the shadows. And Aarav knew that the battle to protect the world from the chaos Samir had set in motion was just beginning.

Chapter 15

Echoes of the Past

The stillness of the compound was almost unnerving as Aarav and Kiara surveyed the aftermath of the battle. The dust, the blood, the devastation everything pointed to one irrefutable truth: the battle had been won, but the war was far from over. Samir Ahmed was dead, but his network had not been eradicated. As Aarav stared at the smoldering ruins, he realized that their success today might only be a brief reprieve before something far worse began to take shape.

Kiara had already begun collecting the data from the wrecked communications center. Her fingers moved quickly, extracting what remained of the key files and sending them to secure servers for further analysis. Despite everything that had happened, she was still focused on her calm demeanor, a stark contrast to the chaos that surrounded them.

Aarav paced restlessly. He had been part of so many operations, so many missions, but this one felt different. They had stopped Samir's plan in its tracks, but there was a gnawing feeling in his gut that they hadn't yet reached the heart of the conspiracy. Other powerful players had supported Samir from the shadows. He had barely scratched the surface of what had been set in motion.

"Aarav, you need to see this," Kiara's voice broke through his thoughts.

He moved quickly to her side. The screen in front of her displayed new data, a complex array of encrypted files, names, and hidden networks. It was a patchwork of global influence financial transactions, covert meetings, coded communications between multiple countries, and something even more troubling: connections to the very institutions that had been responsible for regulating global peace and security.

"This isn't just a terror network," Aarav muttered, eyes scanning the information. "This is a global syndicate. A shadow government operating from the inside."

Kiara's expression grew darker. "Exactly. They've infiltrated every level of intelligence agencies, political institutions, and even economic powerhouses. Samir was just in front. The real power has been pulling the strings from behind the scenes for years."

Aarav's mind raced as he tried to process everything. This was worse than he had imagined. They had exposed a faction that had been grooming itself to take control of global governance. And Samir had been their chosen tool, a puppet who had been disposed of when he outlived his usefulness.

"They're still out there," Aarav said, his voice cold. "And now, they'll be even more dangerous without Samir. They'll go underground, reorganize, and come back stronger."

Kiara looked up from the screen. "What do we do now?"

Aarav exhaled slowly, his eyes narrowing. "We hunt them down. We find the key players, the ones pulling the strings. But we need more. We need names. We need to know who is still in control."

That night, as the moon hung low over the desolate landscape, Aarav couldn't shake the feeling that something far darker was on the horizon. They had won a battle, yes but it was only one of many. The conspiracy was vast, and it was clear now that Samir had been just the tip of the iceberg. Aarav had been chasing shadows, but the shadows had turned into a deadly storm that was about to swallow everything in its path.

The next few days were a whirlwind. Aarav and Kiara worked tirelessly, sorting through the data they had retrieved, and piecing together fragments of information. They reached out to trusted allies within R&AW and other intelligence agencies viz Mossad, CIA, sharing the intel and seeking help to dismantle the far-reaching network they were up against. But each lead they pursued seemed to lead to more questions. The conspiracy was far more entrenched than they had realized, and the people behind it were no ordinary criminals. They were powerful, with resources and connections that reached deep into the core of the world's systems.

The Mossad Connection

The clock on Aarav Menon's wall ticked relentlessly, each passing second a reminder of the mounting pressure he faced in his covert mission to dismantle the syndicate. The stakes had never been higher. As his mind raced through plans and counter-plans, a sudden ping on his encrypted phone broke the silence. A single word flashed across the screen: David.

Aarav's lips curled into a faint, grim smile. He had been expecting this.

David Ben-Ari, a name that Aarav had only heard whispered in the shadows of the intelligence community Mossad's finest, or so the legends went. Known for his uncanny ability to slip into any role and extract the most invaluable of intelligence, David had a reputation that spanned continents. But he was not just any agent; he was a man with a past that, unlike Aarav's, had left him scarred. The stories spoke of a failed mission in Syria, a loss that had turned him from a pragmatic operative into someone far more dangerous detached, calculating, and willing to make ruthless decisions. For Aarav, who had always operated by a code of honor, the idea of working with someone like David was as daunting as it was necessary.

He tapped the screen, reading the message that followed: Meet at the usual place, midnight. Time to end this.

The location was familiar a secluded café in the heart of Toronto's bustling downtown, a place where no one would dare suspect two intelligence officers to be. As Aarav walked through the evening streets, a mix of anxiety and anticipation settled over him. This wasn't just another meeting. This was the moment when their alliance would either solidify or crumble under the weight of their differing worlds.

When he entered the café, the air thick with the scent of brewed coffee, David was already seated in the corner, his face obscured by the shadow of his baseball cap. Aarav approached with the careful step of someone who knew that one wrong move could be fatal.

David's piercing blue eyes met Aarav's, and without a word, he slid a dossier across the table. The silence between them was thick with unspoken history, both men measuring each other up. Aarav opened the file, his eyes scanning the documents. Photos of the syndicate's key players, intelligence on their movements, their hideouts, and most importantly their next big strike. This was it. The breaking point.

"You know, I never thought I'd be working with someone like you," David said, his voice low, the weight of years spent in the shadows evident. "But I suppose when it's all about survival, you take whatever help you can get."

Aarav didn't respond immediately. He had studied David's file every move, every mission. But there was something about the man that didn't add up. The cold exterior, the guardedness it was clear David had seen things that left him with scars no amount of intelligence could heal.

"I don't need to know your story, David," Aarav said, his voice steady. "I just need you to get me the information we need, and help me take them down."

David leaned back, a faint smile tugging at the corner of his lips. "You know, it's not just about the information. It's about timing, precision. This syndicate has more resources than you think. But that's what I do best get in, get out, and leave no trace. But be prepared to burn some bridges. There's no clean way to do this."

Aarav nodded. He had always known that the line between right and wrong blurred the moment you stepped into the world of espionage. But this mission wasn't just about duty it was personal. The syndicate had far-reaching ties, some of which were far too close to home.

The night stretched on as they discussed plans sophisticated, daring operations to infiltrate the syndicate's encrypted communications, take down their financial backing, and finally, track down their leader. David was methodical, precise, and as Aarav watched him work, he realized that the Mossad agent had a certain level of ruthlessness he could never afford to embrace.

"You've got your way of doing things," David said as they reviewed the last set of intel. "But sometimes, you've got to take the gloves off. This is not a game. These people… they'll stop at nothing."

Aarav paused. "And I'll stop at nothing to make sure they pay for what they've done."

David looked up, meeting Aarav's eyes with a rare intensity. "Then let's get this done, Menon. We take down the syndicate. We finish this together.

The next days were a blur of calculated movements, infiltrations, and high-risk operations. Aarav and David formed an unlikely but formidable duo Aarav's disciplined methods complemented by David's unorthodox yet effective tactics. As they tracked the syndicate's financial transactions, hacked into secure communications, and dismantled their network, Aarav found himself learning from David, not just about espionage, but about the deeper costs of a life lived in shadows.

David was, after all, more than just an agent. He was a man who had sacrificed his soul to the service of his country, someone who understood the true meaning of loss. Their growing partnership brought Aarav face to face with the realities of intelligence work, and more than once, he found himself questioning his own choices just as David had.

But there was no turning back now. Their mission was set. The syndicate would fall, and with it, a new chapter in Aarav Menon's life. But for now, he would rely on the man sitting across from him David Ben-Ari, Mossad's best, and his unlikely ally.

One night, while analyzing the data, Aarav stumbled upon something that made his blood run cold: the names of several high-ranking officials who were still active within the syndicate. These weren't just pawns, they were leaders, decision-makers, people who had the ability to bring about massive shifts in global politics.

Kiara leaned over his shoulder as he looked at the screen, her brow furrowed. "This is bigger than we thought. These names… some of them are untraceable. It's like they don't exist."

Aarav's jaw tightened. He didn't need confirmation he already knew. These weren't just criminals or rogue operatives. They were the power brokers, the ones who had been pulling the strings from the shadows for years. And now, they have regrouped. They were ready to strike again.

Aarav couldn't sleep that night. The weight of the mission hung over him like a fog, and every time he closed his eyes, the faces of the people he had lost in this war flashed before him. Srinivas, Samir, even Malhotra he had once trusted these men, and now they were all gone, victims of their ambition, their corruption.

He stared out of the window, his mind racing. There was only one way forward now. He needed to go after the core of the people who had been pulling the strings all along. But they were everywhere. Their reach was global, and they were untouchable, hidden behind layers of secrecy, wealth, and power.

And then, it hit him. The solution wasn't about hunting them one by one. It was about striking at the heart of the network exposing their infrastructure, their connections, everything they had built over the years. If he could unravel the heart of the syndicate, he could collapse the entire operation.

He didn't have the luxury of time. The world was already slipping into chaos, and if he didn't act now, it would be too late.

"Aarav," Kiara's voice interrupted his thoughts, "I've found something. It's not just a lead, it's the blueprint. The syndicate's core structure, their plans for the future."

Aarav stood up quickly, his heart racing. "What is it?"

Kiara's fingers danced across the keyboard, bringing up a series of encrypted files. "It's a meeting. A gathering of the highest members of the syndicate. They're planning something major, something that will change everything. If we intercept this, we can finally expose them all."

Aarav's pulse quickened. "Where is it?"

Kiara looked up, her expression unreadable. "Switzerland. The same place where Samir was operating. It's their central hub."

Aarav exhaled sharply. "Then it's time to finish this." He turned to Kiara, his voice steady but filled with determination. "We're going to Switzerland. We stop this before they can make their move."

Chapter 16

The Final Blow

The private jet touched down at Zurich Airport just before dawn, its landing lights slicing through the frigid alpine darkness. Aarav Menon, David and Kiara Mishra descended the airstairs briskly, their movements fluid, purposeful, and cloaked in the shadowy garb of seasoned operatives. The frosty Swiss air stung their faces, but neither flinched. Ahead lay their target a heavily fortified mansion nestled in the outskirts of Zurich. Here resided the nerve center of the global syndicate, their last stronghold.

This was not just an assignment; it was the culmination of months of relentless pursuit, subterfuge, and personal loss. Aarav, the deep-cover Research and Analysis Wing (R&AW) operative masquerading as an academic, knew that the hourglass of destiny had emptied its sands. Tonight, they would deliver the final blow with the help of the formidable Mossad, the institute.

Zurich's cobblestone streets gave way to dense forests as the duo navigated toward their objective in a modified Land Rover Defender. The vehicle, laden with tactical equipment, was an unassuming beast bulletproof, EMP-resistant, and fitted with a concealed weapon cache.

Aarav reviewed their plan one last time, his voice steady despite the stakes.

"Kiara, we breach at 0400 hours. Primary objective: retrieve the intel from the mainframe. Secondary objective: neutralize Vladimir Krane and his top lieutenants. The extraction point is three clicks east; the chopper is on standby. Call sign: Falcon. Clear?"

Kiara nodded, her hands deftly assembling a Heckler & Koch MP5 submachine gun. "Crystal clear. But Aarav, Krane is a fox. Don't underestimate him. He'll have contingencies."

Aarav smirked, checking his SIG Sauer P320 sidearm. "So do we."

The mansion loomed ahead like a fortress of avarice, surrounded by dense pines and patrolled by syndicate guards armed with FN SCAR rifles and night-vision goggles. The perimeter bristled with motion sensors, infrared cameras, and a razor-wire fence.

Aarav and Kiara, clad in matte-black combat suits lined with thermal insulation, approached from the north flank, taking advantage of the terrain's natural depressions. Aarav deployed a signal jammer from his tactical belt, disrupting the perimeter's surveillance grid for a narrow two-minute window. They scaled the fence silently, landing cat-like on the other side.

The first guard never saw it coming. Aarav's suppressed knife glided through the cold air, embedding itself into the man's neck. Kiara neutralized the second with a swift takedown maneuver, muffling his death throes with surgical precision.

Their comms crackled softly. "Perimeter secure. Moving to Phase Two," Aarav whispered.

Inside the compound, the duo maneuvered through labyrinthine hallways, relying on blueprints obtained during a previous mission in Prague. Kiara hacked the first layer of the mansion's security system using a pocket-sized Raspberry Pi device. The red dots of laser tripwires flickered and died.

"System disarmed," she murmured.

The grand meeting hall was bathed in the golden glow of an opulent chandelier, its light mocking the clandestine darkness in which the syndicate thrived. At the center, a mahogany table stretched like a warship, occupied by seven men who had dictated the fates of millions. At the helm sat Vladimir Krane, the mastermind of the syndicate, a man whose name was whispered in fear across continents.

Aarav and Kiara took their positions, hidden in the shadows. Aarav's heartbeat remained steady as his eyes fixed on Krane. The Russian oligarch, dressed in a bespoke suit, exuded an aura of invincibility. But tonight, he would bleed.

"Gentlemen," Krane's gravelly voice filled the room, "our operations in Asia and the Middle East remain intact, despite the recent setbacks. The data leaks were unfortunate, but our contingencies are in motion. Soon, we will have global economic leverage."

Aarav's voice, cold as a blade, interrupted the villainous soliloquy. "Leverage, Krane? You mean chaos."

The room froze. All eyes darted toward Aarav as he stepped into the light, his pistol aimed squarely at Krane's chest. Kiara flanked him, her MP5 at the ready.

Krane's lips curled into a sardonic smile. "Ah, Agent Menon. I've heard much about you. The ghost of Delhi, the man who buried Samir. But you're too late. You see, power is not seized by exposing secrets. It's seized by eliminating threats."

Krane's hand moved beneath the table. Aarav fired instinctively, the bullet grazing Krane's shoulder. Chaos erupted as armed guards stormed the room, engaging the duo in a blistering firefight.

"Cover me!" Aarav shouted as he flipped the table for cover.

Kiara's MP5 spat fire, her aim unerring as she took down three guards in rapid succession. Aarav lobbed a smoke grenade, the room filling with a dense cloud that disoriented their adversaries.

"Switch to thermal," Kiara ordered, activating her goggles. The guards, now blind, became sitting ducks. Aarav's SIG Sauer barked repeatedly, each shot finding its mark.

Krane, clutching his bleeding shoulder, retreated towards a concealed escape hatch. Aarav pursued, his movements relentless, while Kiara held the line against reinforcements.

The escape hatch led to an underground tunnel system, dimly lit and echoing with the sound of Krane's hurried steps. Aarav followed, his breathing controlled, his weapon raised. The tunnel smelled of damp earth and treachery.

Krane, realizing escape was futile, stopped abruptly and turned, a Desert Eagle .50AE in his hand. The two men faced each other, the air between them crackling with tension.

"You don't understand, Aarav," Krane said, his voice dripping with desperation. "This isn't about money or power. This is about control. Order. Without us, the world will descend into chaos."

"Save your philosophy," Aarav retorted. "Your order is built on blood and lies. And tonight, it ends."

Krane fired, the deafening roar of the Desert Eagle reverberating through the tunnel. Aarav dove to the side, the bullet narrowly missing him. He returned fire, his shot piercing Krane's thigh. The oligarch collapsed, his weapon clattering to the ground.

Aarav approached; his pistol trained on the fallen man. "For every life you've destroyed, for every lie you've told this is justice."

Aarav emerged from the tunnel carrying a USB drive containing the syndicate's entire operational framework, retrieved from Krane's encrypted watch. Kiara was waiting at the rendezvous point, her face smudged with soot but victorious.

"Mission accomplished?" she asked, her voice tinged with relief.

Aarav nodded, handing her the drive. "The world will know everything."

As they boarded the extraction chopper, the mansion erupted in flames, a self-destruct mechanism triggered by Krane's last act of defiance. Aarav watched the inferno from the air, his expression unreadable.

The Aftermath: A New Beginning

The revelations from the USB drive Aarav Menon had risked his life to retrieve not only reshaped geopolitical dynamics but also etched an indelible mark in the annals of covert operations. Powerful men and women fell like dominoes as their dark secrets spilled into the public domain. The media's cacophony of breaking news and exposés was a testament to the sheer magnitude of the operation. Yet, amidst this global turbulence, Aarav and Kiara remained unseen, their roles erased from the narrative.

In his modest yet serene apartment in New Delhi, Aarav sat at his desk, gazing out of the window. The city's vibrant hum contrasted sharply with his silent contemplation. The mission was over, but the scars it left were profound. His body carried the physical bruises of battle, but it was the emotional toll that weighed on him more. He clutched the cup of chai Kiara had handed him earlier. The warmth seeped into his palms, a grounding reminder of life's simple pleasures.

Kiara stood across the room, leaning casually against the doorframe. She observed him with a mixture of pride and concern. "You've been sitting there for hours," she said, breaking the silence.

Aarav turned, offering a faint smile. "Reflecting. We've won a battle, Kiara, but the war… it's endless."

She walked over, placing a comforting hand on his shoulder. "That's the thing about wars. They're fought in shadows by people like us, so others can live in the light. And Aarav, thanks to you, that light is brighter today."

Aarav reached up, covering her hand with his. "Thanks to us, Kiara. I couldn't have done this without you."

The camaraderie between them was undeniable, forged through fire and shared peril. But Kiara's path was different now. She had chosen to step back from the field, a decision Aarav both respected and envied. As they talked, the sound of approaching footsteps caught Aarav's attention.

Aanya appeared at the doorway, her presence transforming the room. Dressed in a simple kurta, she radiated an elegance that was both understated and arresting. Her smile was the anchor Aarav didn't realize he needed.

"There you are," she said, walking over to him. Her tone was warm, her affection unmistakable.

Aarav stood, setting his chair aside. "And here you are," he replied, a softness in his voice reserved only for her.

Aanya stepped closer, wrapping her arms around him from behind. Her cheek pressed against his back, and she exhaled deeply, as though letting go of the weight of the world. "Ready for your next lecture, Professor Menon?" she teased.

Aarav turned within her embrace, his eyes locking onto hers. "Always ready, Professor Aanya Menon," he countered, his lips curving into a playful smile.

Aanya laughed, the sound like a melody that filled the room. Her laughter faded as Aarav leaned in, his lips brushing hers with a tenderness that spoke of unspoken promises and unwavering devotion. The kiss deepened, a dance of passion and love, each moment a reminder of what they had fought for and what they had found in each other.

The two had married quietly days ago, in a ceremony attended only by close friends and family. It was a union that symbolizes resilience, a coming together of two souls who had faced life's harshest trials and emerged stronger. Their bond was a sanctuary, a refuge from the storm of espionage and chaos that had once defined Aarav's existence.

Their apartment reflected their shared life. The bookshelves were filled with tomes on international relations, history, and management testaments to their shared intellectual pursuits. A small photo frame on the mantelpiece held their wedding picture, both of them radiant with joy.

Aarav held Aanya close, his fingers running through her hair. "You've made all of this worth it," he murmured.

Aanya tilted her head, her eyes shimmering with emotion. "And you've shown me what it means to truly live, Aarav."

They sat together on the couch, the conversation flowing seamlessly between mundane topics and profound reflections. Aanya recounted her day at the university, weaving tales of her students' quirks and her latest research projects. Aarav listened intently, his laughter echoing hers, their connection palpable.

Later that evening, they walked onto their balcony, the city's skyline illuminated by a myriad of lights. Aarav stood behind Aanya, his arms encircling her waist as they gazed at the world below.

"You know," Aanya began, her tone contemplative, "sometimes I wonder if we'll ever truly leave that world behind the one you were so deeply entrenched in."

Aarav tightened his hold on her, resting his chin on her shoulder. "It's a part of me, Aanya. It always will be. But being with you has given me something I never thought I'd have a reason to hope, to dream beyond the mission."

Aanya turned to face him, her hands resting on his chest. "Then promise me something," she said softly.

"Anything," Aarav replied without hesitation.

"Promise me that whatever comes next, we'll face it together."

Aarav's gaze didn't waver. He cupped her face in his hands, his thumbs brushing away a stray tear. "I promise, Aanya. Always."

As the night deepened, they returned inside, the warmth of their home a stark contrast to the cold winds outside. Over dinner, they shared stories, laughter, and quiet moments of understanding. The television played in the background, a news anchor discussing the global upheavals caused by the recent revelations. Aarav muted it, choosing instead to focus on the life he and Aanya were building.

When they finally retired to bed, the world outside seemed distant, almost irrelevant. Aanya rested her head on Aarav's chest, her hand tracing patterns over his heart.

The room was bathed in the soft glow of moonlight, casting an ethereal luminescence upon the couple. Aanya lay nestled in Aarav's embrace, her breath mingling with his. His fingers traced gentle patterns along her skin, a silent language of love.

"Do you think we'll ever have a normal life?" she whispered, her voice barely audible.

Aarav chuckled softly, his lips brushing against her temple. "Normal is overrated. Besides, with you, every day feels extraordinary."

Anya smiled, her eyes fluttering closed. She was content in his arms, the world outside fading into insignificance. Aarav leaned in, his kiss soft and tender. As their lips met, a spark ignited, igniting a fire within them.

With a gentle touch, he unraveled her from the blanket, their bodies naked and vulnerable. He traced the contours of her body, his fingers lingering on every curve. Aanya shivered, her skin tingling with anticipation. His touch was a symphony, a melody that resonated deep within her soul.

As he moved closer, their bodies intertwined, a dance of passion and desire. The room filled with the sound of their ragged breaths and the soft rustling of sheets. In that moment, time stood still, and they were lost in a world of their own creation.

A Glimpse of What's Next

Morning sunlight streamed through the curtains, painting the room in hues of gold. Aarav woke to find Aanya already awake, sitting by the window with a book in her lap. She looked up as he approached, her smile brightening the room.

"Good morning, Professor Menon," she greeted.

"Good morning, Professor Aanya Menon," he replied, leaning down to kiss her cheek.

As they prepared for the day ahead, their lives intertwined seamlessly, their partnership extending beyond love into every facet of their existence. Aarav knew challenges would arise, but with Aanya by his side, he felt ready to face anything.

Before leaving for their respective lectures, Aarav paused by the doorway, watching Aanya gather her notes. She looked up, catching his gaze.

"What?" she asked, her tone playful.

"Just marveling at how lucky I am," he said, his voice filled with sincerity.

Aanya walked over, her hand resting on his chest. "We're both lucky, Aarav."

As Aarav stepped out into the bustling streets, a sense of purpose filled him. The battle against injustice was far from over, and he knew the world still needed people like him. But now, he also had something worth fighting for—a life built on love, hope, and the promise of a brighter tomorrow.

And as he walked away, a shadowy figure watched from the distance, a faint smile playing on their lips. The syndicate had been dismantled, but the world of espionage was never truly at peace.

Acknowledgments

First and foremost, I extend my deepest gratitude to the intelligence operatives, those nameless, faceless heroes who work tirelessly in the shadows, ensuring our safety and freedom. Their sacrifices and dedication to duty form the backbone of the story within these pages.

While their identities remain hidden, their commitment to protecting the nation is something I hold in the highest regard, and I hope this narrative does justice to their courage.

To my father, whose courage and discipline in service to the nation continue to inspire me. And to my mother, whose intellect and guidance have always been my guiding light.

To my readers, thank you for joining Aarav Menon on this thrilling journey. Your engagement, your excitement, and your willingness to delve into the world of espionage and intrigue make all the hard work worthwhile.

Lastly, I would like to acknowledge the incredible global network of thinkers, historians, and writers whose ideas and research shaped the background and events of this novel. The richness of international relations, political dynamics, and the complex world of intelligence operations was made accessible to me through your work.

This story would not have been possible without each of you. Thank you.

Glossary

1. ISI (Inter-Services Intelligence)

The intelligence agency of Pakistan is responsible for gathering intelligence, conducting covert operations, and national security. The ISI plays a pivotal role in espionage activities across the region and is often involved in counterintelligence operations against India.

2. R&AW (Research and Analysis Wing)

India's primary external intelligence agency is responsible for conducting espionage, gathering intelligence, and handling counterintelligence operations abroad. RAW operates covertly to protect national security and has been involved in numerous successful operations worldwide.

3. Mossad

The national intelligence agency of Israel is known for its clandestine operations, counterterrorism missions, and the protection of Jewish interests worldwide. Mossad has earned a reputation for precision and efficiency in its global intelligence operations.

4. CIA (Central Intelligence Agency)

The United States' principal foreign intelligence service, is responsible for gathering national security intelligence, executing covert operations, and overseeing international espionage activities in alignment with U.S. government interests.

5. MI6 (Secret Intelligence Service)

The United Kingdom's primary intelligence service is tasked with foreign intelligence gathering, counterintelligence, and covert operations abroad, often working in close cooperation with other global intelligence agencies like the CIA and Mossad.

6. Agent Handler

A case officer or intelligence officer is responsible for managing and guiding the activities of undercover agents or informants. In espionage, the handler acts as a liaison between the spy and the intelligence agency, ensuring their safety and objectives are met.

7. Black Site

A covert facility where individuals are detained outside the reach of international law or public oversight. Often associated with secret interrogations and classified operations.

8. Deep Cover

The practice of embedding an operative within an enemy organization or society while maintaining a false identity. Operatives in deep cover often live under a fabricated persona for years or decades, gathering intelligence and carrying out operations without being detected.

9. False Flag Operation

An operation carried out by one organization or country but designed to appear as though it were conducted by another. The purpose of a false flag operation is to mislead, deceive, or manipulate public perception or political outcomes.

10. Tradecraft

The specialized skills and techniques used by intelligence operatives to gather information, communicate securely, and carry out covert operations. This can include surveillance, encryption, disguise, and dead drops.

11. Dead Drop

A secretive location where information, equipment, or funds are exchanged without direct contact between individuals. Dead drops are often used by spies to avoid detection during exchanges of sensitive materials.

12. Wet Work

A term referring to operations involving assassination or other forms of violence. It is used to describe covert operations where lethal force is applied to eliminate a target.

13. Mole

A spy who infiltrates an organization and works covertly within it to pass information to a foreign intelligence service. Moles often work within an enemy organization for long periods without being detected.

14. Counterintelligence

Activities are designed to prevent or thwart the efforts of enemy spies or to detect and neutralize the efforts of infiltrators within one's organization. This may include surveillance, deception, and psychological tactics.

15. Black Lotus

A code name for a high-stakes operation in the novel. The term symbolizes the elusive nature of the mission, which remains hidden beneath layers of complexity and danger, much like the rare and dark flower.

16. Mission Briefing

A classified meeting or document that provides an intelligence operative with the details of a specific mission. It includes the objectives, intelligence on targets, and protocols for completing the mission.

17. Surveillance

The act of monitoring an individual or location for intelligence-gathering purposes. This can be done physically (through direct observation) or electronically (through hacking or intercepting communications).

18. Asset

An individual who provides useful information or intelligence to an intelligence agency. This can be a source within an enemy organization or even an informant within a country's borders.

19. False Identity

A fabricated personal history or background is usually created for an operative to assume while conducting undercover operations. This identity can include fake documents, histories, and other tools to maintain cover and avoid detection.

20. Extraction

The process of safely removing an intelligence operative or asset from a dangerous situation or hostile environment. Extraction operations are highly risky and require precise planning and execution.

21. Encrypted Communication

Messages that are encoded to prevent unauthorized access. Intelligence agencies rely on encrypted communication systems to protect their operations and ensure secure transmission of sensitive information.

22. Satellite Surveillance

The use of satellites to gather intelligence through imagery or signals intelligence (SIGINT). This method allows intelligence agencies to monitor large areas or specific targets remotely.

23. Safe House

A secure location is used to house operatives, assets, or individuals who need to be protected or hidden temporarily. Safe houses are used during transitions or when an operative needs to lie low.

24. Double Agent

An individual who pretends to work for one intelligence agency while secretly working for another. Double agents can provide misleading or false information to their original agency, often causing confusion or damage to operations.

25. Clandestine Operation

A covert or secret operation carried out by intelligence agencies. These operations are typically high-risk and require careful planning to ensure success while avoiding detection by adversaries.

26. Handler

A person within the intelligence agency who is responsible for managing an agent or operative's missions and ensuring their safety. Handlers are critical to the success of covert operations, providing guidance, resources, and support.

27. Signals Intelligence (SIGINT)

Intelligence is collected from electronic signals, such as communications, radar, or encrypted data. SIGINT is a critical part of modern espionage operations and is often used to track targets and intercept messages.

28. Interception

The act of capturing or intercepting communications, data, or transmissions, is often used in espionage to gain insights into an adversary's plans or activities.

29. Asset Compromise

A situation where an intelligence asset, such as a spy or informant, is exposed or betrayed, often resulting in the loss of valuable information or the termination of the asset.

30. Blowback

A term used to describe unintended consequences that result from covert actions. These can include public backlash, escalations of conflict, or retaliatory actions by adversaries.

31. Psychological Operations (PSYOPS)

Operations are designed to influence or manipulate the perceptions, attitudes, or behaviors of individuals or groups. These operations often target the enemy's morale or public opinion and are a key tool in modern intelligence warfare.

32. Asset Recruitment

The process by which intelligence agencies recruit individuals to become informants or spies. Recruitment can be voluntary or through coercion, depending on the circumstances.

About the Author

Sreeranjan Menon T is an Assistant Professor in Management, with a rich background shaped by his upbringing in a family with ties to the Indian defense services. His father retired from the Indian Air Force, and his mother, a retired professor, instilled in him a strong sense of discipline, intellectual curiosity, and an unyielding commitment to excellence. These formative experiences have greatly influenced Sreeranjan's perspectives, particularly his keen interest in international diplomacy, espionage, politics, and strategy.

A passionate defense enthusiast, Sreeranjan applies meticulous planning, strategic thinking, and foresight to his intellectual pursuits and storytelling. This love for strategy and tactical decision-making is evident in his writing, where every plot twist and character move is carefully thought out, leaving readers on the edge of their seats.

This novel marks his entry into the world of fiction writing, where he combines his interests in espionage and international diplomacy with a flair for thrilling storytelling. Operation Black Lotus is a testament to his ability to blend real-world intrigue with fictional suspense, offering readers a captivating glimpse into the dangerous world of espionage and covert operations.